Rosa and the Daring Dog

megan rix

PUFFIN

PUFFIN BOOKS

UK | USA | Canada | Ireland | Australia
India | New Zealand | South Africa

Penguin Books is part of the Penguin Random House group of companies
whose addresses can be found at global.penguinrandomhouse.com.

www.penguin.co.uk
www.puffin.co.uk
www.ladybird.co.uk

First published 2019

001

Set in 13/20 pt Baskerville MT
Typeset by Jouve (UK), Milton Keynes
Printed and bound in Great Britain by Clays Ltd, Elcograf S.p.A.

A CIP catalogue record for this book is available from the British Library

ISBN: 978–0–241–36914–2

All correspondence to:
Penguin Books
Penguin Random House Children's
80 Strand, London WC2R ORL

I'd like people to say I'm a person who always wanted to be free and wanted it not only for myself.

Rosa Parks

Chapter 1

Detroit, USA

By dawn, the snow's icy white crispness had blanketed the whole city of Detroit. Trucks were laying salt along the streets to stop cars from skidding. Boots crushed the ice on the busy footpaths to slush.

A small brown-and-white pit bull terrier puppy with bright blue eyes raced out into the whirling whiteness as soon as the back door was opened. His paws sank into the snow and he shook his tiny body, sneezing with excitement.

Then he opened his mouth and stuck out his little pink tongue to catch a falling snowflake. The wind blew the flakes in circles in the air and he raced after one and then another, barking, as he tried to catch them. He rolled over and over in the snow until his fur was soaked through and then he jumped up and chased the flakes again.

'Be quiet!' a harsh voice shouted from the kitchen. But the puppy was too excited to stop. There were snowflakes everywhere!

He yelped when a rough hand grabbed him by the scruff of his neck.

'I told you to be quiet!' another angry voice shouted at him.

The puppy struggled to break free, his small paws scrabbling in the air.

The man's sandalwood-and-cedar cologne filled the puppy's nostrils and the little animal whimpered in fear.

*

On the other side of town, the sound of excited laughter rang out as children crossed the park next to Birwood Elementary School.

'Look out!'

A snowball flew through the air, splattering against the side of the six-foot-high concrete wall at the edge of the park. The wall ran across the back edge of the park and the school playground and then along the bottom of the gardens on the street. Sparkling snow had settled on the top of the wall and beside it, small eager hands scrabbling to roll it into more icy missiles.

Eddie pulled back her bedroom curtains to wave at her mum and dad as they headed through the snow to board the number 41 bus to work. It would carry them to the River Rouge Ford car factory as it had every weekday since Eddie had started school. They caught the bus early every morning and it bore them

3

home late every evening. Two months ago, in December, Eddie had gone with her parents on the bus to the factory's Christmas party. She'd counted forty stops until they'd finally arrived almost an hour later.

She watched the bus draw up, saw her mum and dad board, and as it pulled away she hurried to get ready for school. *Can't be late for breakfast club*, Eddie thought with a nervous leap in her stomach. Today was project day.

The puppy didn't know how long he'd been inside the trash can, but it felt like forever. His owner had bundled him into the trunk of a car, before roughly taking him out in the park and dropping him in the bin. The puppy had fallen asleep on top of the empty drinks cartons and candy wrappings while he was waiting for his owner to come back. But now he was awake again, and his little black nose started sniffing around. Sticky bits of bubble gum . . . nothing interesting there. He ignored the empty chocolate wrappers and instead sought out a bit of mouldy pizza that he could smell right at the bottom of the trash can. It was gone in a gulp, followed by some forgotten french fries and a leftover bite of a burger. But it wasn't enough to fill his empty belly. He lay down, shivering.

An hour later, the puppy woke again at the sound of a bell. His tongue was dry and he licked his lips. He was *so* thirsty.

The bell was soon followed by the noise of excited children playing in the snow-covered schoolyard next to the park. The puppy yapped and yapped, begging to be let out of his metal prison. His tender paws scrabbled desperately, scraping against the icy cold tin. His nose nudged at the lid and a blast of fresh air ruffled his fur. But he was too small to move the lid any further. He stretched up to the narrow opening, panting, but the rubbish beneath him gave way and he fell back down. He stared up at the unreachable blue sky with wide eyes. The school bell rang again, the sounds of the children soon stopped, and all went quiet. The puppy whimpered, curled up again among the rubbish and fell into a long, fitful sleep.

Chapter 2

That afternoon, inside Birwood Elementary School, Eddie was sitting on her hands to stop herself from biting her nails. Nearly all of the other children in her class had already presented their first project of the year and it was soon to be her turn. Their projects were on America in the First World War, and they'd all been working on them since last year – since the 11 November to be exact. Eddie knew Miss Rodriguez had picked that date because it was the anniversary of the end of the war, which had happened way back in 1918. The eleventh hour of the eleventh day of the eleventh month.

For project day, Miss Rodriguez had put American flag bunting all round the classroom. It made Eddie think about what the streets must have looked like on 11 November 1918 – celebrating the soldiers returning home to their families in triumph. Some children had come in home-made First World War costumes and others had worn clothes from the dressing-up box that was kept beneath the school stage.

Eddie shifted in her seat and looked around the room as she waited for her turn. Olivia's project had been about the food that American soldiers ate during the war. Her mum had even sent in some doughnuts – which Eddie and the rest of the class thought was a very good idea.

'Women volunteers took doughnuts to the front lines to give the American soldiers a sweet taste of home,' Livvy said, as Eddie and the other children munched.

'Is that why they were nicknamed "doughboys"?' Eddie asked.

Livvy shrugged and Miss Rodriguez smiled. 'Good question, Eddie! But no – that name dates back to the time of the Civil War. It was either because the foot soldiers used to polish their belts with flour or because their buttons looked like dough. No one's really sure.'

Eddie loved listening to everyone else's presentations in Miss Rodriguez's class. So far she'd learnt about famous people from the First World War and heard some sad stories about horses and mules that were sent to the front line. One of her classmates had done a presentation on a pigeon called *Cher Ami* who'd saved lots of American soldiers; another had talked all about the clothes people wore during the war.

Harry, who was on the seat next to Eddie, licking his sugary fingers, asked, 'What else did the soldiers eat?'

'Tinned food mostly, and hard biscuits and coffee, tins of corned beef and then chocolate and doughnuts,' Livvy told him.

'Doesn't sound too bad,' said Harry.

'*I'd* like the chocolate and doughnuts,' Joshua said from the back of the room.

'Now, who would like to go next?' Miss Rodriquez asked.

Eddie bit her bottom lip and stared down at her desk so she wouldn't be picked. She *did* want to tell everyone about her First World War project, but she *didn't* like having to stand at the front. She was sure she was going to forget what she was supposed to say with everyone staring at her. So far she'd managed not to be chosen. The only problem was the longer she waited the more nervous she felt.

'Harry,' Miss Rodriguez said. 'Are you ready to give us your presentation?'

'Yes, ma'am' Harry said enthusiastically. He pushed his round-framed glasses up his nose, high-fived a glum-looking Eddie and swaggered to the front of the room.

Eddie shook her head in disbelief and envy as she watched him. Wasn't he even the slightest bit nervous?

Harry stuck a poster he'd drawn of some soldiers and medals on the board, grinned at everyone and began.

'In 1917, black American soldiers were fighting for the right to be counted as citizens of the country they were born in. My project is about the Harlem Hellfighters – a daring regiment of black men who won the French

Croix de Guerre medal.' He pointed to the paper medal he'd pinned to his sweatshirt. 'These soldiers were also known as the "Men of Bronze". They were proud to be Americans and proud to be black. They spent one hundred and ninety-one days in the front-line trenches and never lost a foot of ground. At the end of the war every member of the regiment was given a *Croix de Guerre* medal by the French government. The Harlem Hellfighters ended up coming home as one of the most decorated units in the entire army. There was a parade along Fifth Avenue in New York for them!'

Harry held up a picture of a smiling man in uniform. 'One of the Harlem Hellfighters, Henry Johnson, suffered twenty-one wounds and rescued another soldier while stopping an enemy raid in the Argonne Forest in 1918.'

'Wow!'

'He's amazing.'

Harry grinned at the class. 'He was.'

'Thank you, Harry,' Miss Rodriguez said.

Harry took down his poster from the board and headed back to his seat.

'I expect you all know from your research that over a million African Americans came forward to fight in the First World War,' Miss Rodriguez told the class. 'They hoped the war would bring true democracy to America, and end segregation and racism as well. They hoped it would give them the right to vote.'

'It didn't, though, did it, miss?' said Livvy, her fists clenched. 'After the celebration of their return there was the Red Summer of 1919 and race riots.'

Miss Rodriguez nodded. 'You're right, Olivia. But even though the First World War was a terrible conflict, it marked a big step forward and a turning point in African-American history.'

It was almost home time. Eddie was the only one left who hadn't shared a project.

'Edna,' Miss Rodriguez said, 'are you ready?'

Eddie swallowed hard and nodded. Then she stood up and went to the front of the class, clutching a rolled-up sheet of paper.

She tried to quash the last of her nerves. She had done her project on famous dogs from the war – she loved dogs and wanted the rest of her class to hear all about them. Hands shaking a little, she stuck her poster to the board and pointed to the first photograph.

'This is Sergeant Stubby, a stray pit bull Boston terrier cross, who became a war hero,' she said softly. In the picture, Sergeant Stubby was wearing a special dog coat decorated with lots of medals that had been made for him in France.

'Louder, please, Edna,' said Miss Rodriguez with a smile.

Eddie took a deep breath and pointed to another picture, this time of a German Shepherd with his head tilted to one side. 'This dog was named Rin Tin Tin by the soldier that found him as a puppy. Rin Tin Tin went on to become a Hollywood film star after the First World War.' Eddie pointed to a picture of a small, scruffy dog. 'And finally, little Rags was a stray mixed-breed terrier who was found by some American soldiers on a street in Paris. They called him Rags because they thought he was a bundle of rags when they first spotted him.'

'He's cute,' Livvy said.

'All dogs are cute!' Eddie told her with a grin.

'Thank you, Edna,' Miss Rodriguez said, when Eddie had finished. 'That was very well done, especially once you spoke up. And thanks to all of you for your wonderful presentations today. I've learnt lots and I hope you have too.'

'I liked the doughnuts best, miss,' Josh said.

'Me too,' said Harry.

Eddie took her seat, feeling warm. That hadn't been so bad after all. *Next time*, she thought, *I'll volunteer at the beginning.*

'For our second project of the year I want you to find out all you can about someone very special. Someone whose birthday it was yesterday.'

The children looked at each other. *Sunday 4 February?* It hadn't been any of *their* birthdays.

'Was it your birthday, Miss Rodriguez?' Eddie asked.

The teacher laughed and shook her head. 'No, this is someone *really* famous. I'll give you some more clues. She'll be seventy-seven years old this year. She was born in Alabama in 1913 . . .'

'Before the First World War even started,' Aldo said, and Miss Rodriguez nodded and continued.

'Her first name begins with the letter "R" and she's probably most well known for refusing to give up her seat on a bus . . .'

Now everyone knew the answer and hands flew up into the air.

'Rosa Parks!' The children shouted together.

Miss Rodriguez smiled. 'Yes. Your new project is on Rosa Parks, the mother of the civil rights movement in the USA. She was told to give up her seat on the bus because she was black. When she refused, she started the Montgomery Bus Boycott that became a huge movement against racism.' She held up a book and Eddie squinted to see the cover. There was Rosa Parks, sitting on a bus.

'We'll be reading this autobiography that Mrs Parks wrote, as well as writing and performing a play about her for the whole school and your parents to watch to celebrate Juneteenth.'

Every year the children in the Fifth Grade performed a play about a famous African American to celebrate Juneteenth. Juneteenth, or Freedom Day as some people called it, celebrated the end of slavery in the USA back in 1865. Last year, the play had been about a lady called Sojourner Truth, and there'd been lots of food and dancing and singing. Now it was Eddie's class's turn.

'Who's going to play Rosa Parks?' Livvy wanted to know.

'We'll decide that tomorrow,' Miss Rodriguez told her.

'Can my grandma and grandpa come to watch?' asked Robin.

'Absolutely,' said Miss Rodriguez.

'Are we writing the play ourselves?' Eddie asked, and her teacher nodded.

The class was still buzzing with thoughts for their new project when the home-time bell rang.

'See you tomorrow, Eddie,' Harry said as he swung his bag on to his back.

'Yeah, see you,' Eddie said. But she wasn't leaving school just yet.

The puppy yapped desperately from his tin prison when he heard the children heading home through the park.

'Can you hear a dog?'

'Sounds like it's coming from one of the houses behind the wall.'

'I bet it wants to come out and play!'

The puppy kept on yapping, getting more and more desperate. Its paws scrabbled at the

tin. Its nose pushed against the trash-can lid.
But no one came to let him out.

'Let's make a snowman.'

'I want to play snow angels.'

The children laughed as they darted around
in the snow.

Gradually the sound of voices died away
and so the puppy stopped barking too. He was
now very cold and very hungry. But worst of
all was the thirst. His nose and gums were
dry. He licked at the cold tin of his trash can
prison, whined and closed his eyes.

Chapter 3

Eddie never hurried home from school because she knew there wouldn't be anyone there when she got in. Her mum and dad worked long hours at the car factory and then they had the forty-stop bus ride home too.

'Can I help take down the bunting?' she asked Miss Rodriguez.

'Oh, yes, please – thanks, Edna – and I want to put up everyone's posters and drawings from the First World War project.'

There were already a lot of pictures stuck to the walls of the classroom. As well as students' artwork there was a poster of the United Nations Universal Declaration of Human Rights, and encouraging quotations from famous people.

Eddie stuck Harry's poster beside a quotation from Frederick Douglass.

'Once you learn to READ, you will be forever FREE.'

Everyone at Birwood Elementary was very keen on reading. They even had a small library full of books that parents and grandparents helped to run. Some of the books had been bought with money from home-made cake stalls and a school disco, and others were the children's own books that they'd brought from home to share with their friends.

'I thought you gave your presentation very well today, Edna,' Miss Rodriguez said gently.

'Thank you, ma'am.'

'Once you got started you were on a roll. I don't know why it took you so long to volunteer!'

Eddie grinned and shook her head as she stuck Olivia's poster of doughnuts next to a quotation of Oprah Winfrey's.

'The biggest adventure you can ever take is to live the life of your dreams.'

'I was frightened,' she admitted.

'A little stage fright is necessary if you're going to give a good performance,' Miss Rodriguez told her.

Once the posters were all up, Miss Rodriguez bade Eddie farewell and went home. But Eddie didn't.

Outside in the corridor, the cleaners were mopping the floor. Eddie walked as close to the edge as she could so she didn't mess up their work.

'Did you have a good day, Eddie?' Jade asked her. Jade was nineteen and shared the after-school cleaning with her aunt Coral.

'Yes, thanks! Our next project's going to be on Rosa Parks,' Eddie said.

'Rosa Parks – now that will be interesting!' Coral said.

'Brave lady,' said Jade.

'She'll never stop fighting until there's equality in America,' Coral told Eddie.

'I applied for a Rosa Parks scholarship when I was at high school. Didn't get it, though,' Jade said sadly. 'That money would have been a huge help.'

'You always were smart at school,' Coral said. 'Your mother was so proud of your school reports. I remember her saying she should frame them and put them up on the wall. But that was before . . .' Coral trailed off and Eddie knew she was thinking about the illness that had taken Jade's mother a few years before.

'What would you have used the scholarship money for?' Eddie asked.

'To go to Tuskegee University and learn how to be a veterinarian,' Jade told her with a sparkle in her eyes.

'So you love dogs too!' Eddie said, smiling.

'Not just dogs,' Coral told her. 'Jade was always rescuing one animal or another when she was younger. Do you remember that abandoned raccoon cub you found?'

Jade grinned and nodded while Eddie stared at her, open-mouthed. She hadn't known Jade rescued animals.

'And that possum!' laughed Coral. 'It caused absolute havoc in the house!'

Jade smiled and turned back to her work. 'Those days seem like a long time ago now,' she said, mopping intently at a dirty spot over by the door.

Eddie saw Coral's lips press closely together as she looked at Jade and, leaving them to it, she set off in the direction of the canteen to see if Mrs Hulu needed any assistance. Sometimes Eddie helped put the cutlery away or get things ready for the next day.

'I'm all done, thanks, Eddie,' Mrs Hulu said, when Eddie popped her head round the door. 'But you could take these sandwiches and an apple to Mister Jones.'

'Yes, Mrs Hulu,' Eddie said, as she took the plastic plate.

Eddie found Mr Jones the elderly janitor up a ladder replacing a light bulb in the hall.

'How did your project go?' he wanted to know. 'Did you speak nice and slow like I told you to?'

Eddie nodded but then realized that Mr Jones couldn't see her because he was twisting the light bulb into place.

'Yes – I tried to speak slowly,' she said, 'but talking about dogs from the First World War made me want a dog of my own *even more* than before.'

'Well, why don't you ask your parents if you can have one, then?'

'Oh, Mr Jones, you *know* my mum and dad won't allow a dog in the house. They'll never listen.' She held up the plate. 'Mrs Hulu asked me to bring you this apple and a sandwich. There's some pickles too.'

'Mrs Hulu's always trying to feed me up,' Mr Jones chuckled, and Eddie grinned because Mrs Hulu was always trying to feed *everyone* up. 'I think it's a leftover from when she was put in an internment camp as a child back in the Second World War.'

Eddie nodded. Mrs Hulu had told her class about it when they were doing their project on the Second World War in Fourth Grade. Her family had been sent to the camp when Mrs Hulu was only three years old and not set free again until after the war was over.

'Press the switch to see if the light's working now, would you?' Mr Jones said.

Eddie put the plate with the apple and quartered sandwich on the floor and ran over to press the switch. The hall was immediately flooded with light.

'Our next project is going to be on Rosa Parks,' Eddie told Mr Jones as he climbed down the ladder. 'Did you know it was Mrs Parks's birthday yesterday? She's seventy-seven years old!'

'Was it indeed?' Mr Jones said. 'Well, happy birthday, Mrs Parks. I met her, you know. A long, long time ago now. I don't expect she'd remember me because she meets so many people. But I'll never forget her. So determined!'

'Where did you meet her?' Eddie asked. She wondered about including an interview with Mr Jones as part of her project. It would mean she wouldn't have to do so much talking herself!

'Why, right here in Detroit! She lives here, you know.'

'Does she?'

'Uh-huh. Has done since 1957. I first met her way back in 1963, long before you were born,' Mr Jones continued, as he took one of the sandwiches and offered the plate to Eddie, who took one too.

'Thanks.'

'It was during Detroit's Walk to Freedom march,' Mr Jones said round a mouthful of sandwich.

'What were people marching for?' Eddie asked, as she bit into the soft bread.

'We were protesting about the inequality between races in housing, education and wages. Mrs Parks said it wasn't fair that black families weren't treated the same as white families. Hundreds of thousands of us marchers there were! Reverend Martin Luther King led the way and Rosa was right there in the front with him.'

'Did you get to meet Reverend Martin Luther King too?' Eddie asked excitedly. That would be brilliant to include in her project too.

'No, but I heard him speak – and once you had you never forgot it. We lost a great man when he was killed. After he was shot there were riots everywhere!'

'I don't understand why anyone would want to shoot him when he was just trying to make things better for people,' Eddie said.

'I know,' Mr Jones agreed sadly. 'I always like to read a few of his speeches on Martin Luther King Day. "*The time is always right to do what is right*" – that's one of my favourites.'

Ever since Eddie had started school, everyone in the country had the third Monday in January as a day off to commemorate Reverend King's birthday and to celebrate his life.

But her new project was on Rosa Parks and she wanted to find out more about her.

'So what did you say to Mrs Parks when you met her?' Eddie asked.

'Well, when I met her the Detroit sky had just turned cloudy and so I offered her my umbrella just in case it started to rain. She was all dressed in her Sunday best clothes for the march, just like the rest of us. I wasn't worried about a little rain getting on me, but I didn't like to think of her getting wet.' Mr Jones took a pickle and bit into it with a crunch. 'You want the other pickle, Eddie?'

'No – you have it.'

'Don't mind if I do.'

'Weren't you scared you'd be arrested for marching and protesting?' Eddie asked.

Mr Jones's brow wrinkled as he remembered the march long ago. 'You can't let being scared stop you from doing what's right, Eddie. Here, do you want the apple?'

Eddie nodded. 'Thanks, Mr Jones.' She put the apple in her pocket as they headed down the corridor to the coat hooks.

'My grandaddy used to grow the best apples when we were children. My brothers and sisters used to eat them before they were ready, so sometimes they were sour, but mostly they were as sweet as sugar and the juice from them would run down your chin. Had to watch out for wasps, though – they're awful fond of apples!'

'Did you ever get stung?' Eddie asked. She thought that a wasp might not be too pleased with someone biting into its apple.

Mr Jones shook his head. 'Nope, never been stung by a wasp . . . almost been stung by a bullet a few times, though.'

Eddie wasn't sure if Mr Jones was joking or not but she hoped he was! She pulled on her coat and took the woollen hat her grandma had knitted from the pocket and pulled it down over her ears. She loved talking to Mr Jones and always felt disappointed when it was time to go home.

'Cold out there,' Mr Jones said, 'and dark too. Here, take this with you.' He pulled a small flashlight from his overalls. 'You can give it back to me tomorrow. Like as not there'll be more snow then.'

'Thanks, Mr Jones,' Eddie said. 'See you in the morning.'

Chapter 4

The puppy was feeling very weak. It no longer tried to get out of its tin prison. It didn't even have enough energy for barking and whining any more. Far, far away in the distance it heard someone singing. Its sensitive ears twitched. It sounded like the person was munching on something. The puppy's stomach growled. The flicker of a flashlight made patterns across the top of the trash can lid where he'd moved it a crack. The puppy didn't even raise its head.

Eddie was very glad Mr Jones had leant her the flashlight because although it was only just after five o'clock, it was very dark and a bit creepy as she crossed the park. She'd ended up staying longer than usual because she'd wanted to hear more about the Detroit march from him.

She steeled herself. *Be brave like Rosa Parks!*

Eddie picked up the lid of the trash can by the wall to throw the apple core away – and was amazed to see something furry inside it. If she hadn't had the flashlight she might have thought it was a raccoon cub or a possum like Jade had rescued, but when she shone the light on it she could see that it was a puppy.

'Oh, oh, oh, what are you doing in there?' she said, as its little blue eyes flickered feebly open. Maybe it had crawled inside to escape the cold and got itself stuck.

With the last of its strength the puppy lifted its head and gave a sad little whimper.

Eddie knew dogs could bite because her mum and dad were always warning her about them.

'Never go near a stray dog.'

'They could bite you at any moment!'

'Even if the dog looks friendly, don't get too close . . .'

But this dog was so small, just a baby. She lifted it out of the bin and held it close. The puppy was freezing cold and very floppy. She'd never held a puppy before, but she was sure that something was very wrong.

'Who could have left you in there?' Eddie said. It was obvious now that the puppy was too small to have jumped into the trash can and got stuck there by itself. Eddie looked back at the school. The lights were still on. Mr Jones, Mrs Hulu, Jade and Coral must still be inside. Of course! *Jade!* She'd know what to do. Eddie ran back to the school with the much-too-still puppy in her arms.

Mr Jones, Mrs Hulu, Jade and Coral were in the canteen chatting when Eddie burst in.

'Eddie – are you OK?'

'What's wrong?'

'What's that?'

'It's a puppy! I found a puppy in the trash can over by the wall in the park,' Eddie gasped, as the little dog's head lifted and then flopped. 'I don't know . . . I don't know . . . if it's going to be OK.'

'Here,' Jade said, taking the puppy from her, 'let me see him.'

The puppy made little crying sounds that tore at Eddie's heart.

'Ssssh, ssssh, sssh,' Jade half sang to him as she held him close. 'You're all right now. We've got you.'

'He felt so cold,' Eddie said, and Jade nodded.

'Maybe wrap him in this,' Mrs Hulu told Jade, holding up a hand towel.

'Thanks,' Jade said, taking the towel from her and wrapping it round the puppy. 'He'll probably be very thirsty. Dogs, especially young ones, can get dehydrated even more quickly in cold weather than hot.'

'I didn't know that,' Coral said. 'You'd have thought it would be the other way round.'

Jade shook her head.

Mrs Hulu put a bowl of water on the ground and Jade knelt down with the puppy and held him close to it so he could drink.

They all watched as the puppy lapped.

'That's a good sign,' Jade said. 'A very good sign.'

'How about some food?' Mrs Hulu asked Jade.

'A little scrambled egg, maybe,' Jade told her.

'Coming right up.' Mrs Hulu took some eggs out of the fridge and started to whisk them.

'He'll be OK, won't he?' Eddie asked. The puppy was barely moving, although at least his head was now up as he looked at his rescuers.

'Yes, I think so,' Jade said, as she gently rubbed him with the towel. 'He's a lot warmer than before.'

Eddie reached out to stroke the puppy's head and his little tongue licked her hand.

'I think he's saying thank you,' Jade said, and Eddie smiled. 'If you hadn't found him, Eddie . . . well, I'm not sure how much longer he'd have lasted. It would be very, very cold for a little puppy in a trash can in the snow at night.' Her expression darkened. 'I can't believe someone would throw their puppy away like this. It's awful!'

As soon as the scrambled eggs were cool enough for him to eat, the puppy wolfed them down.

'Another very good sign,' Jade laughed, as the puppy looked down at the now empty bowl and then up at her as if to say "More, please".'

'I can make him some more, no problem,' Mrs Hulu said. 'We have lots of eggs.'

But Jade shook her head. 'Let's see how those settle in his tummy first.'

'You know such a lot about dogs,' Eddie said.

Jade smiled as she stroked the puppy softly. 'I volunteer at the animal shelter near the high school when I'm not working. I love it.'

'You'd have been an amazing veterinarian,' Coral said sadly.

Jade shook her head. 'Sometimes what you thought you were going to be doing with your life isn't what you end up doing. And being here and able to look after this little one is all that matters at the moment.' The tiny puppy looked like he'd fallen asleep in Jade's arms.

Jade smiled at Coral and her aunt smiled back.

'I wish I could take the puppy home,' Eddie said. 'But my mum and dad said I could never have a dog.'

'I'll take him home with me for tonight,' Jade said. 'To make sure he's OK. And I'll get my friend who's a nurse at the animal shelter to check him over. But I'll have to bring him back to school early tomorrow morning while I do my factory cleaning job. I won't be allowed to take him with me and he's too young to leave all by himself.'

'I can keep an eye on him here during the day,' Mr Jones said.

'And I can feed him – we've got lots more eggs,' Mrs Hulu said.

'And I'll get to school extra early so I can take him for a walk – or a cuddle if he's not strong enough for a walk,' Eddie said, as the puppy woke up and blinked at her.

'I think you'll be surprised how quickly this little one will bounce back,' Jade laughed, as the puppy tried to lick her chin.

Eddie looked up at the clock on the wall and bit her bottom lip.

'I'd better be heading home. I told Mum and Dad I'd make dinner,' Eddie said. Her parents loved it when she cooked for them – even if it was just spaghetti hoops on toast.

'Here,' Mrs Hulu said, taking a pie from the fridge and holding it out to Eddie. 'Just cook up some mashed potatoes and serve them with some of this leftover vegetable pot pie from lunch.'

'Are you sure?' Eddie said.

'Yes, I'm sure. A puppy rescuer deserves pie.'

'Thanks, Mrs Hulu.'

Eddie gave the puppy one last stroke.

'See you in the morning, sleepyhead. Bright and early.'

She was so glad that he was going to be OK.

As Eddie walked towards the door, the puppy turned his head and made a funny little sound, somewhere between a howl and a whine.

Once she was outside, Eddie switched on the flashlight and started to jog along the path beside the high concrete wall. She was so excited about finding the puppy that she wasn't frightened of the dark any more. Now it felt magical. The snow on the trees glistened like diamonds under the bright light of the flashlight.

She didn't dare to run too fast in case she dropped the pie but it was almost six o'clock now and her parents would be back soon.

When she arrived home, Eddie dropped the flashlight into her coat pocket, pulled out the key that hung from the chain round her neck and opened the front door.

She'd never made mashed potatoes before, although she'd watched her mum making them. She had an idea in her head that if her mashed potatoes were delicious, it would help persuade her mum and dad to let her keep the puppy. As she peeled the potatoes she thought about what she was going to say. Her parents wouldn't have to do any of the work – she'd do it all, and clean up any messes he made. And if they were worried about how much he'd cost, she could help pay for his upkeep with her birthday and

Christmas money. Maybe she could start running a lemonade stall, or help people clean their windows, or even do their gardening . . .

In no time at all the potatoes were peeled and Eddie set them to boil while she warmed the pie in the microwave. If she'd had time, she would have checked the recipe for mashed potatoes in *The Taste of Country Cooking* cookbook by the famous Southern chef Edna Lewis, but her parents would be home any minute. Once the potatoes were soft, she mashed them up as best she could with a pinch of salt and pepper and a forkful of margarine. She hoped Edna Lewis would approve.

Eddie set the table all ready for her parents' arrival and took three plates from the cupboard. They'd lived in this house ever since she was born. Downstairs there was the kitchen and a lounge with a dining table at one end. There was a green sofa with orange cushions, and a green chair that Eddie's dad liked to sit in with a great big sigh before kicking off his shoes and pulling a book to read from the shelf after a hard day at work. The wallpaper was a faded mustard colour and Eddie thought it must have been original to the house because her mum and dad had done their best to cover most of it up with posters. Nelson Mandela took pride of place on one wall.

'You'd let me keep the puppy, wouldn't you?' Eddie said to his smiling face. Mr Mandela had been locked up in prison in South Africa since before she was born.

Reverend Martin Luther King looked a lot more serious from his spot on the opposite wall. Eddie's mum was always quoting from his speeches just like Mr Jones did. Along the window sill there were lots of photos of Eddie's grandparents, aunts, uncles and cousins, and a few pictures of Eddie as a baby.

Suddenly, there was a blast of cold air as the front door opened, and Eddie heard her mum call out, 'We're home!'

'Something smells good,' said her dad as he came into the kitchen.

'It's veggie pot pie,' Eddie told them. 'Mrs Hulu gave it to us. I did make the mashed potatoes, though!'

'Why did Mrs Hulu give us a pie?' Eddie's mum asked her.

'Because something happened that meant there wasn't time for me to make dinner,' she told them mysteriously.

Her mother and father exchanged a look. 'What happened?' they asked her.

But Eddie just smiled. 'Sit down and I'll bring the food in,' she said.

Over dinner Eddie told her parents about finding the puppy. 'The poor little thing was nearly dead. It probably wouldn't have survived much longer if I hadn't found it in the trash can.'

'Good that you did, Eddie. These mashed potatoes are great,' her dad said.

'Smart of you to take the puppy back to school where they could help it,' said her mum. 'You know I don't think I could have made the potatoes better myself!'

Eddie eagerly tried to persuade her parents to let her keep the puppy. But her mum and dad shook their heads.

'It needs a home,' Eddie said desperately.

'Well, that won't be here.'

'What if it could die if I didn't look after it? Wouldn't you let me keep it then?'

But Eddie's mum and dad were adamant.

'No dogs in this house,' Eddie's dad told her.

'They're so vicious,' said her mum. 'I'd never be able to sleep a wink for worrying it might bite us during the night.'

'Well, that's not very likely, is it?' Eddie scoffed, before she noticed her parents' angry faces. 'Sorry,' she said, looking at her half-empty plate and laying down her fork. She felt deflated. 'I have to do my homework. We're starting a project on Rosa Parks.' She tried to summon up the excitement she'd felt about the new topic earlier, but now all she could feel was sad about the puppy. He needed her.

Her mum and dad looked at each other. Out of the corner of her eye Eddie saw her mum bite her lip and her dad nod his head. Were they going to change their minds and let her keep him after all? Eddie's heart leapt.

'Wait a minute, Eddie . . .'

'We want to explain the reason why we can't let you keep the puppy,' her mum told her.

'We're not being cruel. We really don't think this would be the right place for him to live,' her dad said. 'For a start, we're out all day and a puppy would need company. But that's not the main reason.'

Eddie pushed her leftover food around the plate with her fork. She couldn't think of a single reason why anyone wouldn't want a dog.

'You know how your father and I went to school together in Birmingham, Alabama, where your grandma and grandpa still live?'

Eddie nodded her head.

'Well, in 1963, when we were just ten years old, we were part of the Children's March.'

'There were thousands of us,' Eddie's dad added. 'We went to school as usual, so our parents didn't know what was happening, but then we left our classrooms to march for civil rights. We didn't cause any trouble, all we were doing was marching, but the police hosed us with water, and police dogs bared their teeth and growled at us.'

Eddie's mouth dropped open.

Her mum nodded. 'More than six hundred children were arrested.'

'And we didn't stop – even though we were only your age, Eddie, and we were very, very scared.'

Eddie looked from one to the other. Her poor parents!

'The hoses they turned on us were so powerful they blasted the bark of the trees right off and it's never grown back.'

'I'll never forget those police dogs' teeth. I had nightmares about them for years,' her mum said with a shudder.

Eddie's eyes were wide as she imagined a ferocious dog attacking her mum. 'Did you get bitten?'

Her mum and dad shook their heads.

'No, but we could have been – easily.'

'Now can you see why we can't have a dog in the house, Eddie?'

'But what about a good dog, a little dog – a puppy? There's nothing to be scared of with a little puppy!' Eddie said, but she could see by their faces that her parents weren't going to change their minds.

'No dogs.'

'Please . . .'

'No dogs.'

'It's not fair!' Eddie shouted. She jumped up from the table and ran up the stairs to her room before her parents could see the tears streaming down her face.

Chapter 5

The puppy rolled over and stretched his little paws up in the air.

'Well, good morning to you,' said a friendly voice, and the puppy looked up at the smiling face next to him.

A finger tickled his tummy and he sneezed with delight. The tummy tickling stopped much too soon.

'Time we were going if we don't want to be late,' Jade said, jumping out of bed.

Before he could follow her, she'd scooped him up in her arms and taken him outside to do his business.

'That's it! Good puppy.'

He padded over to sniff at the winter jasmine growing up the wall, but before he got the chance, he was lifted up again and popped on top of a soft blanket in a wicker basket on the front of a bicycle.

'Off we go!' Jade said as she climbed on the bike and pushed down on the squeaking pedals. There was much less snow than there had been the day before.

The puppy sat up in his wicker basket carriage and stared out at the smiling people that they passed.

'What a sweet little dog,' a lady said as they cycled in through the park gates.

'Yes, he is,' grinned Jade.

The puppy wagged his tail. There were so many interesting smells coming from the grass where the snow had melted. But he wasn't brave enough to jump out of the basket when they were going so fast.

They cycled alongside the wall, right past the metal dustbin he'd been stuck in yesterday. The puppy gave a whimper of fear when he saw it, but it was gone in a fraction of a second, and a minute later they'd reached the school.

'What a good puppy you are,' Jade said, lifting him from the basket.

The puppy's shiny wet nose lifted towards the bright blue sky, sniffing at the air.

'You're not strong enough to walk all the way to school yet. But soon you will be and then we won't need my bike. Although cycling is a lot quicker than walking!' Jade told him as they headed in through the rear door of the school.

He gave Jade's face a quick lick as she carried him in through the swing doors of the canteen.

'Well, don't you seem a whole lot better than when you were found?' Mrs Hulu said as soon as she saw him. 'Eddie's going to be very pleased when she sees you looking so well.'

The puppy gazed up at her and wagged his tail as if he were agreeing.

'He's much more alert too,' Jade smiled. 'My friend from the animal rescue centre checked him over last night and pronounced him healthy.'

'Oh, that is good news. Do you think he'd like some scrambled eggs for breakfast?' Mrs Hulu asked.

Jade nodded. 'And maybe a little chicken for lunch – nothing too fatty or salty.' Jade gave the puppy a stroke. 'Meeting you has made me want to work full-time with animals more than ever,' she told him as he rolled on to his back for another tummy rub. 'You be good now. I'll be back at three p.m.' Jade said as she tickled him.

'Have you got time for a coffee or a bite of breakfast before you go?' Mrs Hulu asked her.

Jade glanced at the clock on the wall and shook her head. The puppy sat up and looked at her with his head tilted to one side. 'No time – tell Eddie and anyone else who plays with him not to get him overtired – he's been through a lot and isn't very strong yet. Oh, and we should probably give him a name!' She kissed the top of the puppy's furry head. 'Goodbye, little one.'

The puppy ran after her as she headed for the swing doors – and then sat down in surprise with a yap of protest when Jade disappeared through them.

A moment later, Eddie came racing in. She'd hardly been able to sleep last night because she'd been so worried about the puppy and so sad that she couldn't keep him. As soon as she'd heard her parents leave she'd jumped up and ran out of the door. Now, in the canteen, she stopped when she saw the puppy, a giant smile lighting up her face.

'Hello!' she said, crouching down and stretching her hands out to him.

The puppy almost danced over to her, his tail wagging happily. Eddie hugged him to her and he gave her face a lick.

Mrs Hulu had finished making the scrambled eggs and handed the bowl to Eddie.

'Make sure it's cool before you give it to him. I need to prepare the food for the school breakfast club now,' she said. The children were starting to arrive and Eddie could hear them chatting excitedly in the dining hall. Her tummy rumbled.

The puppy looked over at the scrambled eggs and gave a yap as if he knew the food was for him and he'd like it *now*.

Eddie dipped her finger into the eggs to check. They were still too hot. 'Not yet! We don't want you burning your mouth.'

The little puppy looked at the bowl, then he looked at Eddie and then he opened his mouth to howl in protest.

Eddie laughed and laughed at the funny noise. She thought he sounded like a mini werewolf. 'Little Howly!' she said. She picked up the bowl and blew on the eggs. 'That'd be a good name for you.'

The puppy threw back his head and howled again.

'Jade said be careful not to overtire him as he's not all that strong yet,' Mrs Hulu said, coming back in to get the fruit for the breakfast club.

But Eddie had never had a dog so she didn't know how much was too much. Maybe Howly would let her know somehow.

She dipped her little finger into the egg again. It felt lukewarm – surely it wouldn't burn Howly's mouth now. The puppy stood on his back legs and trotted in a little circle of excitement as the bowl came towards him.

'Yes, yes, it's for you,' Eddie laughed. Howly was trying to gobble up the eggs before she'd even put the bowl on the floor.

'Nice to see such a healthy appetite,' a voice behind them said, and Eddie grinned up at Mr Jones.

'Howly's got that all right!' Eddie told him.

More children and staff were arriving for the breakfast club and it would be hard to keep the puppy hidden for long.

'I'd better take Howly out to do his business,' Eddie said once he'd finished his scrambled eggs. Mr Jones went with her and they both watched as he sniffed at the snowdrops poking through the leftover snow on the grassy area.

'I can look after him while you have your breakfast and then go to class, Eddie,' Mr Jones told her.

'Are you sure?' She really didn't want to leave the puppy.

'Yes, he'll be fine with me, don't you worry,' Mr Jones said, as Eddie gave Howly one last stroke.

'I've got to go,' she told him.

As she walked away Howly gave a yap as if to say *Please don't go*.

'I'll be back soon,' Eddie promised.

Chapter 6

An hour later, Eddie was listening to Miss Rodriguez reading to the class from a book about Rosa Parks when a small brown-and-white puppy came running in through the open classroom door.

'Where on earth . . .' Miss Rodriguez said.

'Howly!' Eddie cried. The puppy looked over, gave a yap of happiness, and then came running to his friend.

'He's so cute,' Harry said. 'Here, puppy!'

But although the little dog looked over at Harry, he didn't want to leave Eddie.

'Is it your puppy?' Miss Rodriguez asked, confused.

Eddie shook her head as she lifted the puppy up and set him on her lap. 'Howly's not really my dog – although I'd like him to be. I found him after school yesterday. He was crying in a trash can next to the big wall! *In the snow!*'

Miss Rodriguez shook her head. 'That's terrible. Who could have done something like that?'

'I don't know,' Eddie said as Howly did his best to lick her chin.

'Lucky you found him,' Harry told her.

Eddie nodded as Howly started wriggling to get down.

'No wonder he loves you so much!' said Livvy.

Eddie put Howly on the floor and he proceeded to sniff at her trainer laces.

'Why'd you call him Howly?' asked Robin.

'You'll know when you hear him howl!' Eddie laughed, as Howly's little teeth clamped on to one of her laces. He tugged at it, making little growling sounds, while the children and Miss Rodriguez watched.

Eddie grinned. She felt more confident when Howly was around. Braver too.

'Could he be our class dog?' she asked Miss Rodriguez.

'I'm not sure,' Miss Rodriguez said, frowning, as she looked at the rest of the children who were all nodding.

'We should have a class dog just like the one on that TV show last week!' Tammy said.

'The dog that saved the whole school?' said Harry excitedly.

Miss Rodriguez frowned again. 'Well, I'm not sure. This is a very *real* puppy.'

At that moment Mr Jarvis, the head teacher, walked into the classroom, followed by a slim elderly lady with grey hair pulled up in a bun. Her brown eyes smiled at the children from behind large-framed glasses.

Eddie's first thought was, *I wonder who this is?* Closely followed by, *I hope she likes dogs!* The lady looked a bit like the picture on the front of the Rosa Parks book that Miss Rodriguez had been reading. Eddie's brow furrowed – actually, she looked a lot older than that.

Mr Jarvis opened his mouth to say something, a big smile on his face, but at the same moment little Howly went running over to him, wagging his tail. Mr Jarvis's eyes crinkled at the corners and his smile grew even bigger.

'Who's this?' Mr Jarvis said, kneeling down to give Howly a stroke.

'Howly!' the children cried.

'Eddie came across him in a trash can in the park after school yesterday,' Miss Rodriguez said, shaking her head. 'Someone had dumped him there.'

'He'd be dead if Eddie hadn't found him,' Harry said.

The woman with the glasses looked very sad. 'How awful,' she said. 'Poor little puppy.'

Howly looked up at her and wagged his tail as if he were agreeing. But the lady didn't reach down to stroke him like Mr Jarvis had, and Eddie wondered if she was a bit nervous of dogs.

'He's very friendly,' Eddie told her.

'Yes, I'm sure he is,' the lady smiled. 'I just didn't expect to see a dog at the school!'

'There isn't usually,' Eddie said.

'But there should be!' Harry said, grinning at the head teacher.

Mr Jarvis chuckled as Howly cuddled up to him. 'He is very cute.'

Then Howly sniffed at a pencil that had been dropped on the floor, picked it up in his mouth and dropped it next to the lady's foot.

'Oh, is that for me? Thank you,' she said.

Eddie grinned.

As the lady took the pencil, Howly gave her hand a lick. She squeaked a little in surprise and then laughed.

Howly trotted back to Eddie and then dived under the desk, having spotted an eraser on the ground. He picked it up and dropped it next to Mr Jarvis.

'Good puppy, Howly!' Eddie laughed.

The dog looked at Eddie and wagged his tail while the head teacher tickled him behind the ears.

'Miss Rodriguez, could I have a word, please?' Mr Jarvis said. Howly trotted after him as he approached the teacher.

'These First World War projects look very interesting,' the lady said, while the head teacher and Miss Rodriguez spoke in soft voices. She was looking at the displays on the wall that Eddie had helped Miss Rodriguez to put up.

'That's mine,' Harry told the lady when she stopped in front of his poster of the Harlem Hellfighters.

'Brave men,' she said.

'And this is mine,' Eddie said proudly.

She pointed to the poster she'd made of three famous American dogs from the First World War, and the picture of Sergeant Stubby wearing his special coat of medals that she'd cut from a historical magazine.

'Oh, who made him that?' the lady asked, looking closely at the image of Sergeant Stubby. 'It looks like a fine piece of needlework.'

'Some women in France,' Eddie said.

'Looks like it's made from chamois,' the lady commented. She glanced at Eddie and her eyes were twinkling. 'Years ago, I used to work full-time as a seamstress, and I still like to make things in my spare time.'

Howly ran over to Eddie, stood on his back paws and put his front paws on her legs. She picked him up and rubbed her face against his soft fur.

'I can see you love him very much,' the lady said.

Eddie nodded. 'I do.'

Mr Jarvis and Miss Rodriguez were still discussing something. Eddie could see her teacher was smiling and looking excited. She was aware that they kept looking over at her and the puppy, and hoped they were agreeing to keep Howly as the school dog.

'There you are!' Mr Jones said, bursting into the classroom and pointing at Howly. 'I've been looking for him everywhere. I just closed my eyes for one second and the next thing, he'd disappeared! I guess he was wondering where you were, Eddie. Probably wanted to play. He's certainly much more lively than when you found him!'

'So, er, Howly was in school yesterday too?' Mr Jarvis said from the front of the classroom. He didn't sound cross. Eddie had never known Mr Jarvis to be angry about anything. He often said if you had any problems, his door was always open and you could come and talk to him about them.

'Yes, sir, after Eddie found him on her way home,' Mr Jones said.

'I took him back to school because he was so floppy and I was scared he wouldn't survive. Jade knows lots about animals. She was going to be a vet, but she didn't get the Rosa Parks scholarship she needed,' Eddie told him.

The lady with Mr Jarvis looked perplexed. 'I wonder why she wasn't awarded one,' Eddie heard her mutter softly to herself.

Then Eddie took a big breath and turned to Mr Jarvis. 'Could Howly be our school dog, sir? He wouldn't be any trouble and . . .'

Mr Jarvis scratched his head doubtfully and sighed. 'Well . . . I'm not sure. But I do know that before it could even be a consideration, the school board would have to agree, and letters would need to be sent home to parents in case children had allergies or their parents objected. It takes a lot of work to look after a dog, you know. They can be expensive too,' he added.

But Eddie had already thought about that.

'We could raise money to look after him like we raised money for the library,' she said. 'Have lemonade stalls and raffles—'

'We could have a school disco!' Livvy chimed in.

'Cake stall . . .'

'Cookouts . . .'

'Sponsored walk . . .'

'Sponsored silence!'

Mr Jarvis laughed. 'A sponsored silence would be very hard at this school! But Howly would soon be living like a king with all your good money-making ideas.'

'Please, sir,' Eddie said. 'He's a good little puppy and he had such a nasty start in life.'

Mr Jarvis sighed again and rubbed his chin thoughtfully. 'Only yesterday I came across an article about a Reading Education Assistance Dogs trial programme. The idea is to have dogs listening to children reading throughout the country – maybe even the whole world if those running the trial had their way!'

'That'd be perfect,' Eddie whispered.

'How does the programme work?' the lady asked.

'Well-behaved therapy dogs are assigned to a school with their handler and listen to individual children read,' Mr Jarvis told her and the class. 'The schools involved in the trial said the children's reading ability had improved no end since the dogs started coming to them.'

'And the Littlest Hobo was in a school last week,' Robin said. 'And he helped a boy who was in trouble and really sad.'

'That's just a TV show,' Miss Rodriguez reminded him.

'But it's so real!' said Olivia. 'I wish the Littlest Hobo could come here.'

'He doesn't have to, though,' Eddie told her, 'because we have Howly.'

Howly looked up at her and wagged his tail at the sound of his name.

'Yes – that's you,' Eddie laughed.

'I think Howly should be allowed to stay *unofficially* for the time being – now that he's already here,' the lady visitor remarked.

'I think so too, Mrs Parks,' Mr Jarvis agreed, 'although I never imagined us having a school dog before. I *will* have to check with the school board, but one thing I've learnt since working here is to expect the unexpected!'

'Me too,' Miss Rodriguez laughed.

By now everyone in the class except Howly, who'd gone to investigate the interesting smell coming from the wastepaper bin, was staring at the lady with Mr Jarvis. Could she really be *the* Mrs Rosa Parks?

'We're delighted to have you visiting us, Mrs Parks,' Miss Rodriguez said with a smile.

I was right! Eddie thought to herself smugly, forgetting that she'd dismissed the idea almost as soon as she'd had it.

'Mrs Parks?' Mr Jones said, looking as if he could hardly believe his eyes. 'Is it really you? I don't know if you remember, but we met at the Walk to Freedom march – nearly thirty years ago. It looked like it was going to rain and so I—'

'You gave me your umbrella!' Mrs Parks said slowly, reaching back into her memory. She smiled and took his hand, pressing it warmly. 'It was such a kind thing to do. I wanted to return it to you, but with all the crowds . . .'

'Oh no, I didn't want it back,' Mr Jones said, pressing her hand in his. 'I was pleased to think it might keep you dry if needed.'

'It seemed like I was always marching for the cause back then. Not long after the Detroit march I was in Washington, marching again. And then there was the Selma march, of course.'

Mr Jones nodded.

Over by the wastepaper basket, Howly gave a yap as if in solidarity.

'I always took your umbrella with me – just in case it rained – and it often did,' said Mrs Parks. 'I still had it with me six years ago in Washington when we were marching against apartheid in South Africa. I had your umbrella in one hand that day, and a placard in the other, saying, *Freedom Yes. Apartheid No!*'

'Glad to hear my umbrella became so well travelled,' Mr Jones chuckled.

'Thousands of people marching together was a good way to get our voices heard and make sure the powers that be took notice of us,' Mrs Parks said seriously.

Mr Jones nodded. 'Those marches did a lot of good,' he said. 'Things changed.'

'But sometimes they could be dangerous too and people got hurt – or worse,' Mrs Parks added solemnly.

Eddie had been watching Mr Jones and Mrs Parks, but now she noticed Howly instead. He was standing on his hind legs with his front paws on the top of the wastepaper basket.

'Careful, Howly!' she gasped.

But Eddie's warning was too late. The bin tipped over and everything fell out on top of him. Howly sat back in surprise.

'Oh, Howly!' Eddie cried, running over to clear up the mess.

The pit bull's little head bent down and he gobbled up the crust from Miss Rodriguez's breakfast sandwich – a tasty thing found!

'My good friend Mrs Parks said she wanted to meet you all when she heard you were doing a project on her,' Mr Jarvis told the class, as

Eddie put the rubbish back in the bin and carried Howly over to her desk.

'We're delighted to have you here,' Miss Rodriguez said to Mrs Parks. 'Actually, it's such an honour that I almost couldn't believe it!'

'Well, here I am – in the flesh,' Mrs Parks said, pretending to give herself a pinch.

Eddie gave Howly a stroke as he sat on her lap and watched the great lady.

'Now, do any of you have any questions, or anything you'd like to tell me?' Mrs Parks asked the children. Everyone's hand went up now they knew who she was.

'Do have a seat, Mrs Parks,' Miss Rodriguez said, pulling a swivel chair from behind her desk and pushing it over to the older lady. 'This could take a while!'

'Thank you,' Mrs Parks said, sitting down.

Mr Jarvis joined Mr Jones on the other side of the room, and Howly curled up on Eddie's lap, closing his eyes.

Harry put his hand up.

'Yes?' Mrs Parks said, pointing to him. 'What's your name?

'My name's Harry,' he grinned, 'and I wanted to say happy belated birthday, Mrs Parks.'

'Thank you! I have had a lot of birthdays,' Mrs Parks said with a laugh, 'and I hope to have many more! This year my birthday wish was, once again, that Nelson Mandela would finally be freed from prison.' Eddie thought about her parents and their poster of Mr Mandela. She thought they probably would have wished for the same thing.

Mrs Parks looked out at the sea of hands and pointed to Josh.

'My name's Joshua and I wanted to know what your school was like when you were our age,' he said.

'Well, Joshua, not as warm as this, I can tell you! There was only a small log fire to warm the whole school – and no windows. We only went to school for six months of the year so we could work in the fields for the rest of the time. I was lucky because my mother was a teacher, so I knew how to read before I even went to school.' She looked over at Howly, who'd fallen asleep on Eddie's lap. 'No one had thought of reading to dogs back then, but it does sound like a very good idea.'

Eddie looked at Miss Rodriguez, who was smiling happily. She knew her teacher would thoroughly approve of Mrs Parks's love of reading. Eddie just hoped Miss Rodriguez would agree with Mrs Parks about having a school reading dog too.

'Tell us some of your favourite books, Mrs Parks,' Miss Rodriguez said.

'Oh, there's so many.'

Eddie looked down at the little puppy. Howly's eyes flickered as he dreamt. Then he started making frightened little crying sounds.

'Do you think he's remembering being stuck in the trash can?' Harry whispered to Eddie.

'Maybe,' Eddie whispered back.

All she knew was that the sounds made her heart break.

'I'm an avid reader,' Mrs Parks was saying. 'I always read anything I can get my hands on, even when I don't always agree with the texts.'

Eddie wondered what Mrs Parks was reading that she didn't agree with? She put her hand up and wiggled her fingers because she wanted to ask Mrs Parks what she'd meant, but the lady picked Livvy instead.

'My name's Olivia and I'd like to know where you were born,' Livvy said.

Now Howly's little paws started twitching.

Eddie thought maybe he was running in his dream, running from whoever had tried to throw him away.

'I was born in Tuskegee, Alabama, in 1913, Olivia,' Mrs Parks said.

Mr Jones's eyes widened. 'Why, I was in Tuskegee too – during the Second World War,' he said.

'You were one of the Tuskegee African-American airmen?' Mr Jarvis asked, looking very impressed. 'Did you get one of the medals they were awarded?'

Mr Jones laughed and shook his head. 'Sadly not. I was just a kid, not even thirteen when America joined the Second World War, but I was willing to learn so they let me help out at the army field. I did all sorts of jobs.'

Eddie smiled. She looked down at Howly, who was making little snoring noises.

'Was your school just for black children?' Robin asked Mrs Parks.

'Yes, it was, and actually my main school was only for black girls. The Jim Crow laws were in full force then.'

Eddie wanted to know what the Jim Crow laws were. She'd heard the name before, but had always thought Jim Crow was the name of a bird in a book. She waved her hand in the air and then quickly put it down to prevent the sleepy puppy from slipping off her lap. Howly didn't wake.

'So when did school segregation stop?' Harry asked.

'Officially in 1954, Harry, but it didn't stop overnight,' Mrs Parks told them.

'Where I come from in Texas, the schools were segregated too – splitting up the Mexican and white children,' Miss Rodriguez told everyone.

Eddie was surprised she hadn't known this about her favourite teacher. Howly was getting heavy on her lap now, but she didn't want to disturb him. She shifted ever so slightly to look at Miss Rodriguez.

'When my mum was a little girl in Texas, her family had to go to court to protest about school segregation,' Miss Rodriguez continued. 'Back then if you were Mexican there was lots of discrimination. Restaurants wouldn't serve you, and you could only use the swimming pool one day a week! Mexican children were sent to special Mexican schools, but they weren't funded properly and didn't have the good equipment that white schools had.'

That didn't sound at all fair to Eddie.

Matilda, the girl sitting next to Robin, put her hand up. 'My grandma told me she had one typewriter in her whole school and the children took turns to use it. They didn't think it was unfair until they heard about another school for white children that had three *rooms* full of typewriters!'

Miss Rodriguez smiled. 'Fortunately, my family wasn't one of those forced to return to Mexico by Operation Wetback in 1954 – the year before the Montgomery Bus Boycott.' She nodded at Mrs Parks. 'In Texas, a quarter of all Mexican immigrants were forced into boats and out of the country. Some people said we were dirty and disease-ridden, but we weren't! It was just racism. People didn't have a choice, and lots of Mexicans lost their lives because of it.'

Mrs Parks shook her head. 'That was a terrible time and a terrible thing.'

Eddie put her hand up. 'Mrs Hulu in the canteen was once put in a prison camp because she's Japanese-American,' she said.

'Was she? I'd like to meet her,' Mrs Parks replied.

'Mrs Hulu makes the best food in the world,' Livvy told her.

'You're welcome to stay to lunch, Mrs Parks,' Mr Jarvis said with a smile. 'I'm sure Mrs Hulu would be honoured to have you as a guest.'

'I'd like that very much.'

'I'll let her know we've got company,' Mr Jones said, and he slipped out of the classroom, while the discussions continued.

'Were you really tired when you wouldn't give up your seat on the bus?' Livvy asked.

Mrs Parks pressed her lips together. 'No, Olivia, I wasn't just plain tired as people keep saying. I was no more tired than I was on any other day after work. What I was tired of was being downtrodden. My grandmother and mother taught me that all human beings are equal. But on that bus I just knew African Americans like me had suffered too long. When I refused to move on that bus it was because I was sick and tired of being discriminated against for no reason other than the colour of my skin.'

Howly started making little sucking sounds in his sleep as if he were having a big drink of water. Some of the children looked round at the noise. Eddie shrugged her shoulders and smiled.

'I wasn't the only African-American woman who was arrested for refusing to give up her seat on the Montgomery buses in 1955, you know,' Mrs Parks said. 'There was a fifteen-year-old girl called Claudette Colvin earlier in the year, as well as Aurelia Browder, Susie McDonald, who was in her seventies and used a cane to walk, and there was Mary Louise Smith too. They all became plaintiffs in a court battle known as the Browder versus Gayle case to stop the segregation on the buses. The bus boycott started at the time of my arrest in December 1955 and went on until December of 1956, when the court ruled that segregation on the buses in Alabama was unconstitutional. For over a year the Montgomery buses were going up and down the streets with fifty thousand fewer passengers!'

'Were white people angry about the bus boycott?' Joshua asked.

Mrs Parks nodded. 'We did get a lot of hate mail and nasty phone calls, but at least our home wasn't bombed like Reverend Martin Luther King's. My husband Raymond and I both lost our jobs, though, and so we came here to live in Detroit.'

'Were you scared?'

'A little,' said Mrs Parks quietly, 'but I don't feel angry about what happened, just glad it's over.'

The bell rang and made Howly jump. Eddie could feel his little heart thumping very fast.

'It's OK,' Eddie said, giving him a stroke. 'There's nothing to be frightened of.'

'We wouldn't let anything bad happen to you, little puppy,' Harry said, and the rest of the children agreed.

'Maybe you should take Howly outside now – to do his . . . business,' Miss Rodriguez suggested.

'Come on, Howly,' said Eddie.

The puppy hopped off Eddie's lap and headed for the door.

'I love the freshness of the air in winter,' said Mrs Parks when they went outside. 'Oh, look! You've got snowdrops. How pretty.'

'It's overgrown, I'm afraid,' Mr Jarvis said, 'but everything that grows in that soil seems to flourish!

Howly raced over to the grey concrete wall that children were bouncing tennis balls off and tried to catch one. Then he ran over to the basketball court to chase an even bigger ball. The little puppy yapped over and over again, and his tail didn't stop wagging until the bell rang.

'I've so enjoyed visiting your school and meeting you all,' Eddie heard Mrs Parks say to Miss Rodriguez. 'It's such a friendly welcoming place and the children and little Howly are such a joy. But it saddens me to see such a depressing remnant of blatant racism and segregation in your very own playground.'

Eddie looked at Harry, who shrugged. What on earth could she mean?

Chapter 7

'Who would like to play Rosa Parks in our play for Juneteenth about her?' Miss Rodriguez asked after lunch.

Everyone wanted to play Mrs Parks now they'd met her.

'Please, miss, pick me,' Livvy said, waving her hand as high in the air as she could.

'I don't mind just painting the scenery,' Eddie said. Standing up in front of the class was bad enough. Being in a play in front of the whole school and her parents would be much worse!

'Everyone's name should go in the draw, I think,' Miss Rodriguez said. So the children wrote their names on small pieces of paper and folded them in half. Miss Rodriguez emptied out the wastepaper basket and then walked round the room, letting the children drop their folded papers into it.

They all agreed it would be fitting to let Howly pick out a name.

'That's it, Howly!' Eddie said as he put his head in the bin and pulled out a slip of paper.

Miss Rodriguez took the piece of paper from him and laughed when she saw who he'd picked. 'If I didn't know better, I'd say your little puppy could read, Eddie!'

'Why?' Eddie asked.

'Because he's picked you.'

Eddie knew she should be pleased, but she was still worried about having to stand up in front of everyone.

'I'm not very good at learning lines,' she said. 'Maybe someone else should play the part of Rosa Parks.'

'I'll do it!' Livvy said.

But Miss Rodriguez shook her head. 'You'll be fine, Eddie,' she said. 'The best way to combat your nerves is to think about how brave Mrs Parks was and how important her actions were for everyone.'

Eddie nodded. That made sense.

'Don't worry, Livvy, there will be parts in the play for everyone,' Miss Rodriguez said. 'Some of you might have to play two roles!'

'What about Latino people? Where did they sit on the bus? I'm half Latino!' Bianca said.

'And Chinese people? Where could they sit?' asked Minudi.

'What about Native Americans?' said Jack.

'It looks like we're going to be doing lots of research for our projects,' Miss Rodriguez said. 'And I'll be very interested to hear the answers you find to these questions.'

No one wanted to play the part of the mean bus driver.

'But he *has* to be in it,' said Harry.

'Maybe we could make him like a scarecrow or a puppet,' Eddie said. 'Out of straw. He doesn't have to be a real person.'

Eddie looked down at Howly, who'd fallen fast asleep on top of her school bag. At least she wouldn't have to worry about where *he'd* sit on a bus, because Howly was so small she could just hide him in a big bag and no one would even know that he was there.

*

94

After school, Eddie had lots of company as she walked Howly round the playground, his little legs dancing with excitement. It seemed that all the teachers and children from the rest of the school wanted to say hello to the puppy! Eddie and her classmates made sure he wasn't overwhelmed.

'One at a time!' Livvy told them.

'Don't push,' said Harry.

'He's just a puppy,' said Robin. 'He'll be scared if you all crowd him.'

Eddie gazed at Howly, who didn't seem to be scared at all. In fact, he seemed to love the attention.

Livvy and Joshua organized everyone into a queue. Howly looked up at the children as they each gave him a stroke.

'Next,' said Joshua, after the First Graders all had a turn, and the next group stepped up.

When it was time for everyone to go home, it seemed like Howly had been stroked by hundreds of people. He looked exhausted.

Going back into school, Eddie and Howly found Jade in the corridor. She was opening an envelope with a nervous look on her face. Then, as her eyes scanned the letter inside, Jade gave a little squeak and put her hand to her mouth.

Howly ran right up to her and put his front paws on her legs so he was as tall as could be.

Jade crouched down to give him a cuddle, holding the piece of paper out of reach.

'Hello, puppy,' she smiled. 'Have you been good?'

'I'm calling him Howly! And, Jade, he's been amazing,' Eddie said, her eyes shining. 'He's been stroked by just about everyone in the whole school! He might even get to be our school Read To Me dog.' She paused, remembering Jade's nervous expression. 'What was in your letter?'

Jade grinned as she ruffled Howly's soft fur. 'A message from Rosa Parks herself – saying she'd like to meet me! She wants to talk about that scholarship that I didn't get.'

Howly tried to snatch the piece of paper from her hand.

'Oh no, Howly, you can't have this,' Jade said. 'Not everyone gets a note from Rosa Parks. I'm going to treasure this forever.'

'That's amazing!' said Eddie, thrilled for her friend. Howly looked at the paper again and whined.

'I'd better be getting home,' Eddie said, giving Howly a stroke. 'Congratulations on that letter, Jade.'

'And I'd better get on with some cleaning,' Jade said. 'Although I'm not sure how helpful Howly's going to be with that!'

Eddie laughed. 'Not very, I bet!'

As she walked back with a spring in her step, Eddie thought about how cross she'd been with her parents the night before. It wasn't their fault that they were frightened of dogs. She felt determined to make it up to them.

When she got home, the first thing she did was pull *A Taste of Country Cooking* from the bookshelf, grinning.

'Something smells delicious!' said Eddie's mum as she opened the front door at half past six.

'What did Mrs Hulu make for us today?' her dad joked as they sat down at the table.

'Not Mrs Hulu,' Eddie told him proudly. 'Me!'

'I had to make it a bit differently because we didn't have all the ingredients,' Eddie said anxiously, bringing through the bowls of sweet potato casserole.

Her parents were full of praise once they'd tasted it.

'This is fantastic, Eddie!'

'You might even be as good as your namesake one day.'

Eddie shook her head, embarrassed. Edna Lewis loved making up recipes and was a famous chef who'd brought Southern cooking to the whole of America. Eddie was just copying her recipes as best she could.

'You know the puppy I found? I'm calling him Howly,' she told her parents as she tucked in. 'Mr Jarvis said he might be able to be our school dog and listen to children read. Howly's so friendly and he's been stroked by just about everyone at school – and he loves scrambled eggs.'

'Sounds like a good puppy,' said her dad.

'So why did you name him Howly?' her mum asked.

'Because he loves howling!' Eddie told her parents, giggling. 'When we all started singing "John Brown's Body" in music class this afternoon, he got so excited that he threw back his head, opened his mouth and started howling along too!'

Her mum and dad laughed at the thought. It had been so funny, Eddie had barely been able to sing. Howly had especially loved joining in with the chorus:

'Glory, glory, hallelujah! Glory, glory,
hallelujah!'
'*Ooooo-oooooooh-oooooooha!*'

Eddie wiped a tear of laughter from her eye at the memory.

'He does seem to make you very happy,' Eddie's dad said, exchanging a smile with her mum.

'Yes, he does,' Eddie agreed with a grin as she scraped her plate clean.

The next day, straight after breakfast club, Mr Jarvis sent round a message that everyone, including Howly, was to come to the school hall straight away.

When Eddie walked in with Howly in her arms, Mr Jarvis beckoned them to the stage. Nervously, Eddie mounted the stairs. As the children came into the hall, they kept looking and pointing at them. Eddie stroked Howly's soft fur to reassure both herself and the puppy. It felt strange having hundreds of eyes staring at her. But Howly didn't seem to mind!

'Now I've heard that lots of you have already met our newest student – little Howly. Do you like him?' Mr Jarvis asked when everyone had sat down.

The children were all nodding and grinning and so were the teachers.

'Put your hand up if you'd like Howly to be here every day as our school dog,' Mr Jarvis said.

Eddie was amazed. Every single hand in the room was up.

'Put your hands up if you think you'd read more if you were allowed to read to Howly,' Mr Jarvis said.

Everyone's hands went up again.

'That's all I needed to know,' Mr Jarvis said. He reached out a hand to pet Howly, who gave an excited bark. 'I'll be taking your opinions to the school board as soon as I can arrange a meeting with them – and I might take little Howly with me too.'

Chapter 8

Every day for the rest of the week Howly woke up to Jade's smiling face. And every day he got to ride in his basket through the park to what he thought must be the best place in the whole world.

'It's just like he was always supposed to be here,' Eddie said, as she and Mrs Hulu watched the puppy wolfing down his morning scrambled eggs, then looking up at them with a wag of his tail as if to say *thank you*.

'Having Howly here makes our school happier,' Mrs Hulu agreed.

The neighbourhood policeman, Officer Chester Baines, fell in love with Howly too when he popped into the school for a coffee during breakfast club.

'What a sweet little puppy!' Chester said, as Howly gave his face a lick.

'His name's Howly,' Eddie told him, 'because he makes the cutest little howling sounds.' When she related the story of how she'd found Howly dumped in a trash can in the snow, Officer Baines shook his head.

'People's cruelty to animals never ceases to amaze me. Thank heavens there are good folk like you out there too, Eddie.'

Every morning Howly visited one class for a short time and every afternoon he visited another, so all the children got to know him. But the rest of the time he spent either with

Eddie's class or 'helping' Mr Jones. He often fell asleep under Eddie's desk in the soft dog bed that a friend of Miss Rodriguez's had gifted to the school.

'He's such a good little puppy,' Miss Rodriguez said to Eddie late on Thursday afternoon as they cleared up the classroom after lessons.

'Everyone who meets him loves him,' Eddie smiled as Howly picked up a pencil from the floor and brought it over.

'And he hasn't had a single *accident* in school, has he?' Miss Rodriguez said.

'Well, he did a wee in the corridor once, but it was next to the girls' toilet so I was able to clean it up straight away,' Eddie told her conspiratorially.

'That's very good for a little puppy, though,' Miss Rodriguez said, laughing. 'My friend who gave us the dog bed was always finding messes around her apartment when her dog was a puppy!'

The door opened and Mrs Emerson, the Second Grade teacher, came in. 'These are for Howly,' she said, holding out her hand. 'The children made them.'

Howly jumped up from his bed underneath Eddie's desk and came running over to Mrs Emerson to say hello.

The Second Grade children had made Howly lots of *Good Luck* cards for his meeting with the school board the next day.

'Everyone wants you to be our school reading assistance dog,' Mrs Emerson told Howly as she gave him a stroke.

Howly wagged his tail and licked her hand.

Eddie arrived at school very early on Friday morning, and once she'd given Howly a cuddle and his scrambled eggs, they went outside for a play. Jade had given him a really good grooming with a soft brush that morning. 'We want him to look extra smart today!' she told Eddie.

When the bell rang, Mr Jarvis came out to find them.

'Come on, little pup,' the head teacher said. 'Time to show the school board that we need a reading assistance dog – and you're the one we want!'

'Be good, Howly,' Eddie told him as she gave him one last stroke before heading into lessons.

Howly ran happily after Mr Jarvis, but then stopped short, quivering. He stared at the metal box on wheels. The last time he'd been in one of those, he'd been thrown in the trunk in the dark. He didn't want that happening again.

Howly whimpered and cowered, as Mr Jarvis opened the car door and bent down to pick him up.

'That's it,' Mr Jarvis said, putting Howly into the footwell of the car.

Howly tried to jump out again, but Mr Jarvis said, 'No, no, you stay inside – you'll be safe there.'

As Mr Jarvis turned on the engine and drove off, Howly started to feel sick. He whimpered again and curled up in a small ball.

'Not far to go,' the head teacher tried to reassure him, but Howly just made sad little whining noises.

He trembled and cried throughout the short journey, and then – just as Mr Jarvis pulled up outside an office building – was sick all over his freshly brushed fur.

*

Eddie couldn't concentrate on her lessons at all. She desperately wanted to know how the meeting had gone with the board.

Eventually the door squeaked open and Howly raced into Eddie's class with his tail wagging.

'How was it?' Miss Rodriguez asked the head teacher.

Eddie expected Mr Jarvis to look happy, but his expression seemed worried. 'It wasn't Howly's best day,' he said quietly to Miss Rodriguez, as the class clamoured to pet the little puppy. Eddie strained to hear more. 'All we can do now is wait to see what the school board decides.'

Eddie bit her lip as she watched Howly bounding around. What on earth could have happened?

Chapter 9

SUNDAY 11 FEBRUARY 1990

On Sunday morning there was a knock at the front door.

'Who can that be?' Eddie's mum said. She still had her dressing gown on.

'It's for me,' Eddie said, pushing her arms into her coat sleeves. 'Me and Jade are taking little Howly for a walk!'

She opened the door and crouched down to say hello to the puppy. Howly was so excited to see her that he licked and licked her face. Jade giggled.

'Eddie, don't you bring that dog in here.'

'He's showing us his teeth!'

Eddie's parents had appeared behind her.

'No, he's just smiling,' their daughter told them earnestly. 'He smiles a lot!'

Howly wanted to go inside and say hello, but Eddie thought it was best not to.

'Come on, let's go to the park,' she said. The last of the snow had melted and there was a bright, fresh chill in the air.

When they arrived, Howly's nose went straight down to sniff at interesting spots on the grass.

'He looks a lot healthier now than when I found him,' Eddie smiled.

'Yes, and a lot bigger too with all the tasty food that Mrs Hulu's been feeding him,' Jade said.

Eddie laughed. 'Howly does love his food and Mrs Hulu does seem to love feeding him up!'

Suddenly, the puppy gave a yap of excitement and went running towards the high concrete wall at the edge of the park. Eddie glanced over and saw that Josh, Robin, Livvy and Matilda were there. They looked up at the sound of Howly's barks and Eddie gave them a wave.

'What are you doing here?' she asked when they reached them.

'We're seeing where the wall goes after it leaves our school playground,' Josh said.

'Mrs Parks told me it was a segregation wall . . . but it doesn't seem to be segregating anything,' said Livvy.

'Really?' said Eddie, thinking back to the day Mrs Parks had visited. Was that what she'd been referring to when she'd mentioned a 'remnant of blatant racism' in their own playground?

'Mrs Parks would be the one to know!' Jade told them. 'She worked for more than twenty years here in Detroit to improve the housing situation for black people. If anyone knew what that wall was for, it would be her!'

'It goes right along the back of our playground, and along the gardens of the houses next door too,' Eddie said, as they walked alongside the wall. 'Do you know anything else about it, Jade?'

Jade shook her head. 'Sorry,' she said. 'As far as I know it's just always been there. I do remember someone climbing up it and falling off once – broke their arm!'

When Howly saw the trash cans by the wall, he ran past them as quickly as he could. But then he saw a squirrel and chased that instead until it disappeared up a tree. He stared into the branches for a little while and then went scampering after Eddie.

'Squirrels can be very tricky,' she told him, laughing, as another squirrel ran in front of him and then darted up a tree, and stared down from the branches.

Howly looked up at the squirrel and gave a yap.

Eddie and her friends followed the wall along the park and past the houses. Some sections had graffiti on them, but most of it was just a plain greyish-white. It started on Pembroke Avenue and stopped just before Eight Mile Road.

'So it's about half a mile long,' Robin said, as they headed back to the park. They asked everyone they met, but no one knew when or why the big wall had been built.

'It's just always been there . . .'

'Don't remember it being built . . .'

'Doesn't seem any reason for it . . .'

'When we were kids, we liked to climb on it . . .'

'Someone fell off it once . . .'

'. . . and broke their arm!' said Jade. 'I remember that.'

Just then, they heard cheering and shouting coming from the nearby houses. The next moment people came running out, calling to their neighbours.

'What's happening?' cried Matilda. Howly was jumping around in excited circles at the noise. Loud music started playing and people were slapping each other on the back and shaking hands. Cars drove down the road tooting their horns – and in what seemed like no time at all there was an impromptu party going on in the park. Howly ran over to another, much bigger, dog and they touched noses to say hello. Soon they were running about together, playing chase and yapping in delight.

'What's going on?' Eddie called to a couple dancing nearby, wrapped up in their winter coats.

'Nelson Mandela's been freed!' the man shouted.

'Wow!' Jade and Eddie said together.

Josh punched the air. 'I'll bet Rosa Parks is pleased!' he said.

'He's finally been released after twenty-seven years,' a woman told Eddie as tears ran down her face. 'I hardly dared believe that this day would finally come.'

Eddie grinned and thought of her mother and Mr Jones quoting the great man – *As Mr Mandela said himself, it always seems impossible until it's done!*

Eddie could hear the music thumping loudly from her house before they'd even reached the front door.

'See you tomorrow,' Jade told Eddie with a grin, as Eddie gave Howly a goodbye stroke.

'We're celebrating Nelson Mandela's release!' Eddie's mum shouted to her over the music. 'Our trade union at the car factory's been sending money and pushing for him to be freed for years.'

Eddie's dad swung Eddie's mum into his arms and danced around the room with her. 'Poor man hasn't been seen in public since 1962 when he was put in prison!'

Eddie remembered how they'd watched the world tribute concert to Mandela on his seventieth birthday two years ago. It seemed incredible that now he was free at last.

Eddie's mum turned off the music and switched on the news instead. They sat on the sofa and watched as Mr Mandela held up his fist and shouted 'Amandla!' to the people and they shouted back 'Awethu!'.

'What does that mean?' asked Eddie.

'"Amandla" means "power" in Zulu,' her dad told her. 'And "Awethu" means "ours".'

'He's still pressing for an end to apartheid in South Africa,' Eddie's mum said.

'The South African government's effectively built a wall between black and white people,' said her dad. 'If anyone can tear it down it's Nelson Mandela.'

Eddie was just about to ask them about the wall that ran along the bottom of their garden and through the park and school playground but at that moment the phone rang and Eddie ran over to answer it.

'Hello?'

'Eddie!'

Eddie's grandparents spoke at the same time, as usual. Eddie smiled, imagining them with their heads close to the receiver so they could both hear.

'How are you, sweetie?' Grandma asked.

'Did you hear the news?' said Grandpa.

'About Nelson Mandela being freed?' Eddie asked him.

'Oh yes! I'm making a special cake to celebrate,' her gran told her.

'An Edna Lewis cake?' Eddie asked.

'Yes – her famous coconut lane cake.'

'Yum!' said Eddie. 'I wish I could have some.'

'I'll make another one when you come to visit for the weekend over spring break,' her gran promised. 'And you can help me with it, if you like.'

'Yes, please!'

'Been getting good grades at school?' Grandpa asked her. 'You know how important education is.'

'Yes, I got an A for my First World War project and we've just started another one – on Rosa Parks. She came to visit our school because she lives in Detroit now!' Eddie said excitedly.

'She does?'

'And you got to meet her?'

'Yes! And she met Howly, this tiny puppy I rescued.'

Eddie told them about finding the little dog, and then laughed as she recounted the story of his howling along with 'John Brown's Body'.

'We can't wait to meet him,' her grandparents told her.

'He doesn't live at our house,' Eddie told them, unable to stop her voice cracking a little. 'Mum and Dad said he couldn't. So Jade takes him home at night and he's our school dog during the day.'

'Your mum used to love dogs when she was little,' her grandma said. 'And so did your dad. But that was before the Children's March, of course.'

Eddie looked over at her mum and dad. If they had loved dogs once, before the Children's March, perhaps they could be persuaded to love one again.

Chapter 10

Soon wintry February had turned to bright, crisp March, and Little Howly grew even bigger. In every music rehearsal his howl-singing became even louder.

Miss Rodriguez never had to tell the children to smile when they were singing because everyone already was – and they all knew that their school dog was puppy-smiling too.

Mr Jarvis brought in his camera to take a photo of Howly with his mouth wide open and his head thrown back as he howled along.

'I'm going to show this to my family in Louisiana when I visit for spring break,' he said with a smile. 'They'll never believe it!'

'Will your family be coming to see the play for Juneteenth?' Eddie asked him. 'They'd get to hear Howly sing!'

'I think they just might – although they'll have to come all the way from New Orleans,' Mr Jarvis told her.

'It'd be worth it,' Harry grinned. 'Howly should be on TV.'

But Eddie didn't want the puppy heading off to Hollywood. 'He's already a star,' she told Livvy. 'He's the star of our school!'

Howly looked up at Eddie and wagged his tail as if he knew just what she meant.

*

Spring break came round in what felt like no time at all. Although Eddie was looking forward to seeing her grandparents very much, she hated the thought of not seeing Howly's furry face every day.

'I'm going to miss you so much,' she told him on the last day of school as she bounced his ball against the concrete wall and he yapped and chased after it.

Lots of Eddie's friends wanted to have Howly over the holidays, but Jade said she could keep on looking after him at night, and Mr Jones, who lived next to the school and would still be working there during the break, said he'd keep an eye on the puppy during the day.

Mr Jarvis came out into the playground, holding an envelope and a letter. Howly raced over to him with his tail wagging, putting his front paws on Mr Jarvis's trousers and trying to reach the letter, but Mr Jarvis held it out of his way.

'Eddie, I can't find Jade. Would you see if you can locate her and ask her to come and see me in my office?' he said.

Mr Jarvis looked serious and Eddie immediately felt worried. She didn't want Jade to be in trouble.

'Yes, sir,' she said, then ran into the school to find her friend, with Howly in hot pursuit.

Jade was cleaning the girls' toilets.

'Mr Jarvis wants to see you in his office,' Eddie told her.

'OK,' Jade said, peeling off her cleaning gloves. 'You'd better be getting home now, Eddie. It's spring break, after all, and didn't you say you were going to see your grand-parents?'

Eddie nodded, but gave Jade a worried glance. *What could Mr Jarvis want?*

'Don't worry about Howly,' Jade said, misunderstanding. 'I'll take really good care of him while you're away – and I might even let him meet the other dogs and cats at the animal rescue centre.' They headed down the corridor to Mr Jarvis's office together.

'I think he'd like that,' Eddie said. 'He's a very friendly puppy.'

They stopped outside the head teacher's open door. 'Come on in, Jade,' Mr Jarvis said, beckoning her and Howly inside. 'You have a good spring break, Eddie,' he added, and then closed the door.

For a moment Eddie just stared. It must be something very serious if Mr Jarvis closed his door. He hardly ever did that. She could hear his muffled voice from inside and she hesitated – but then remembered her parents had said they were coming home early today. Perhaps they were already there. Eddie walked out of school and headed for home, wishing she'd had a chance to say a proper goodbye to Howly.

When their plane touched down in Birmingham, Alabama, Grandma and Grandpa were waiting at the airport for them.

'How was your flight?' Eddie's gran asked, giving her a hug.

'Good,' Eddie replied. Her nose had been glued to the window for most of the flight, watching the fields and towns they passed far down below.

'Only takes two hours – not like in the old days!' said her dad, as they headed out of the airport.

'It used to take more than eleven hours to drive here from Detroit,' Eddie's grandfather said as they piled into the car. 'And that's if you didn't stop on the way. When we were younger, Eddie, If you wanted to see relatives, especially relatives down South, then you'd need to use a special book to tell you who you could trust and where you'd best avoid.'

'What do you mean?' Eddie asked, as she put her seat belt on. There wasn't much room squashed in the back of the car between her mum and dad.

Grandpa pulled a tattered green paperback pamphlet from the glove compartment and handed it to her before pulling away from the airport.

'It shows all the places that were welcoming to black travellers – places you could eat or get petrol if you were driving, or go to the toilet, or even stay overnight.'

'It was written by a postman, based on his own travel experiences and recommendations,' Grandma told her. 'Soon other black postmen from all over the country were giving their recommendations too.'

'Was there a book like this one for other races?' Eddie asked, thinking about the racism Miss Rodriguez and Mrs Hulu had experienced too.

Eddie's grandfather didn't know. 'Although I did hear Jewish newspapers used to publish a list of places that were welcoming to Jewish people.'

'But why couldn't everyone just go anywhere they liked?' Eddie asked. It all seemed so silly. Eddie saw her grandparents exchange a look, and so did her mum and dad.

'It's much better nowadays,' her mum said, giving Eddie's hand a squeeze.

'Here we are,' Grandpa said, as he pulled up outside their small house not far from the park on Fifth Avenue North. Eddie helped carry the bags inside.

'Mmmmmmm,' she said, as she walked inside and sniffed the air that smelt deliciously of recently baked sweet coconut cake.

Her parents headed upstairs to get changed. They were going to spend the evening with some of their old school friends. Friends who'd gone on the Children's March with them back in 1963.

'That's for desert,' her grandma whispered to Eddie, lifting a Tupperware cake protector to show her the cake lying beneath it. 'But we might save some for your mum and dad for when they get back. Although you'll probably be asleep by then. How about squeezing me a few lemons so I can make some lemonade?'

Eddie nodded and started to cut some lemons in half and then press them on to the glass lemon squeezer, turning it back and forth until she'd got all of the juice out.

Once there was enough squeezed lemons Grandma added the juice to some sugar and water and then added lots of ice.

'Pinch of salt to finish it off,' she said, as she stirred it all together in a glass jug.

Eddie cut thin lemon slices to float on the top of the lemonade.

'See you later, Eddie,' said her mum and dad, coming back downstairs and giving her a hug.

'You look very smart,' Eddie said as they hugged her grandma too.

'Well, thank you,' said her mum.

'We do brush up well, don't we?' said her dad.

'Are we having one of Edna Lewis's recipes for dinner too?' Eddie asked her grandma when her parents had left.

'Yes, we are – but I've adapted it to be vegetarian,' Grandma told her with a smile, as she took down a jar of rice from the shelf. All of Eddie's family was vegetarian. 'I just need to boil the rice and heat up the gumbo.'

'Oh, good,' Eddie said. Spicy gumbo vegetable stew with okra was one of her favourite dishes. 'I love visiting you, Grandma!'

'And I love having you here,' Grandma said, giving Eddie a hug. 'Now why don't you set the table – it'll be time to eat very soon.'

After they'd had dinner and Eddie was feeling very full indeed, Grandma brought in her home-made coconut lane cake.

'This one is the same as the Edna Lewis recipe,' she said, as she cut it into large slices.

Eddie bit into the soft cake. 'This is so good!' she said round a mouthful.

'I'm very glad you like it,' Grandma said.

'Nice to see a healthy appetite,' said Grandpa, and Eddie was reminded of what Mr Jones had said about Howly. The next moment she was telling her grandparents all about the little dog.

'He does sound like an amazing puppy.'

'Not every dog can become a school dog – some would be frightened, or maybe too wild – but your Howly sounds just right.'

'He is,' Eddie agreed.

Eddie loved to look at Grandma and Grandpa's photo albums, especially the pictures of her mum and dad when they were children. Her parents had been next-door neighbours when they were growing up and used to play together all the time.

Each of the albums had the year it was made written on the spine. After dinner, Eddie pulled out the 1963 album and curled up on the sofa with Gran.

'1963 was a very traumatic year for us,' Grandma told her as Eddie turned the pages of the album. This one had newspaper clippings as well as photographs.

'Back then there were no black police officers, firefighters, sales clerks in department stores, bus drivers, bank tellers or store cashiers,' Grandpa said while munching on a second slice of cake.

'That's crazy!' Eddie said. It was hard to imagine what life would be like without friendly police officers like Chester Baines.

'Do you want some more cake, Eddie?' said Grandma.

Eddie shook her head and turned back to the album. 'If I eat any more, I'll explode!'

'Birmingham, Alabama, might as well have been called Bombingham because of all the bomb attacks we used to have back in the sixties,' Grandpa said gravely.

'One of those bombs killed four schoolgirls just across the park from here during a church service in 1963,' Eddie's grandmother said, shaking her head.

Eddie was shocked. 'Who would do something so awful?'

'It was the Ku Klux Klan,' Grandpa said, clearing the salt and pepper shakers from the dining table. 'It was different back then. When the courts said everyone should be allowed in the city parks – whatever their race – Birmingham responded by closing the parks down.' He shook his head.

'So my mum and dad couldn't play in the park across the way when they were children?' she asked. It seemed so unfair.

Grandma gave Eddie a squeeze. 'Time you went to bed,' she said. 'It's getting late.'

As she snuggled under the covers in her cosy attic room, Eddie looked up at her gran. 'I'm glad we can go wherever we like now,' she said.

'Me too,' Grandma said, as she gave her a kiss on the nose. 'We met some good people through that green book, though – people who opened up their houses and fed us without asking for a penny – people who are still our friends to this day.'

'Like Mum and Dad's friends here?' Eddie said.

Grandma nodded. 'Friends through thick and thin.'

Eddie closed her eyes and thought about her friend Howly. She hoped he wasn't missing her too badly. She wished he could have come to her grandparents' house as well. Her attic bed would have been a lot more comfortable with Howly in it too.

Chapter 11

The next morning, Eddie's mum and dad were still in bed asleep when Eddie ate her scrambled eggs for breakfast.

'Howly loves scrambled eggs,' she told her grandma.

She couldn't help thinking how much she missed him and knew he must be missing her too.

Once she'd finished eating, she went with Grandma on the bus to the city.

'I want you to pick out something nice for yourself and I'll treat you to it,' Grandma said to Eddie as they entered a large department store called Macy's. It had a big red star next to its name and Eddie had never been to such a grand shop before.

There were so many interesting things that it was hard for Eddie to decide just what she wanted. She liked clothes, but there were so many toys to choose from as well – soft toys and trucks and games and Disney costumes. A tiara from *The Little Mermaid* movie, decorated with fake jewels, caught Eddie's eye. She wanted to show it to Grandma, but Grandma was looking at some scarves in the corner of the store. Eddie picked up the tiara and hurried over to show her.

'Grandma, look!' she said – but at that moment a hand grabbed her shoulder.

'Where do you think you're going with that?' a security guard asked her.

Fear flooded through Eddie and her heart started to race as she stared up at the huge man. She was so scared that it was even hard to breathe.

'I was going to show it to my grandma,' Eddie said, baffled.

'A likely story.'

At that moment her gran looked round, saw the security guard, dropped the scarf she was holding and gasped. 'Eddie . . . what's going on?'

'I wanted to show you this tiara. It's pretty,' Eddie said. She didn't know why the security guard was being so rude. She held up the tiara so that its fake jewels glistened.

'She was trying to steal it,' the security guard said.

'I wasn't!' Eddie insisted desperately. 'Here.' She gave the tiara back to him with shaking hands. Customers were looking round at them, shocked. Eddie's tummy was swirling with fear, and she felt awkward and embarrassed. 'I didn't do anything wrong,' she said to her grandma, determined not to cry. 'I didn't!'

They left the department store together and Eddie was shocked to see a tear run down Grandma's face.

'What's wrong?' Eddie asked.

'I'd so hoped things would get better one day,' her grandmother said, 'but I really don't know if I'll see the end of racism in Alabama in my lifetime.'

'I wasn't trying to steal that tiara,' Eddie insisted.

'I know you weren't,' Grandma replied, 'but sometimes people just make assumptions based on how a person looks.'

Eddie felt sick. Why would anyone think she would steal, just because she didn't look like them? It wasn't fair. It wasn't right.

'Let's go home and I'll show you how to make some of Edna Lewis's sugar cookies,' Grandma said, squeezing her shoulder.

'Don't tell Mum and Dad what happened,' Eddie said. 'Please.' It would only spoil their holiday.

All the way back on the bus Eddie felt like people were staring at her. She straightened her back defiantly, but she still felt uncomfortable. All she wanted was to be with Howly, giving him hugs and burying her face in his soft puppy fur.

The few days at her grandparents' went by very fast, and in no time at all they were back at the airport, ready to catch the plane home.

'We'll see you in the summer, Eddie,' Grandpa said.

'Bye, Dad,' said Eddie's mum. She gave Eddie's grandma a hug.

'We're looking forward to seeing that little dog Eddie keeps talking about,' smiled her gran. 'What's his name again?'

'Howly,' Eddie said, excitement bubbling up at the thought of seeing him very soon.

'And the play for Juneteenth – you'll be there for Eddie's acting debut?' Dad asked.

'Oh yes! We wouldn't want to miss that.'

Eddie's grandparents gave her one last hug and then it was time to board the plane.

Eddie felt a bit worried at the idea of them seeing her in the school play. She hadn't felt comfortable with everyone staring at her in the shop or on the bus, and she didn't think she was going to like everyone staring at her when she was on stage.

She tried to distract herself with thoughts of Howly. 'I hope he's been OK without me,' she told her mum and dad, as they took their seats on the plane.

'I'm sure he's been fine,' Dad said.

'He's got lots of people to look after him,' said her mum.

Eddie nodded. 'But none of them could love him as much as I do,' she said.

When her mum and dad went to work early the next morning, Eddie made herself breakfast and then headed over to school to see Howly.

Even though it was holiday time, Mr Jones was still working. He was out in the playground, digging, over by the grassy area near the concrete wall, with Howly watching close by.

When Howly saw Eddie, he did a double take and then came running over to her, launching himself into her arms and nearly knocking her over.

'Oh, I've missed you,' Eddie laughed, hugging him. She thought he seemed to have grown even more during the few days she'd been away.

'Not as much as he's missed you!' Mr Jones told her. 'Poor Howly was very confused when you weren't here. Stopped outside your classroom and just looked up at me as if to say, *What's going on?*'

Howly was running round and round in little circles of happiness. He picked up one of Mr Jones's gardening gloves and dropped it next to Eddie.

'Thanks, Howly,' Eddie said, picking it up.

'What are you planting?' she asked Mr Jones.

'Tomatoes here and then some potatoes over there,' he said.

'Can I help?' Eddie asked him.

'Oh yes! If we get them started now, we might have some to eat by the summer.'

When Eddie crouched down and began to dig, Howly got very excited and began digging too, as fast as his paws could go.

'What did Mr Jarvis want to see you about on Friday?' Eddie asked Jade when she found her up a ladder, cleaning the top of the kitchen cupboards.

'Howly,' Jade said, coming down the ladder.

Eddie looked at her nervously.

'The school board wrote to Mr Jarvis saying that they thought Howly was too . . . immature to be a school dog.'

Eddie's heart sank. 'What happened?'

'When Mr Jarvis took him to the meeting, poor Howly was sick all over himself in the car and did a whoopsy in the meeting room. *And* he ran across the conference table and scattered paper everywhere! The members of the school board weren't impressed at all. Mr Jarvis didn't even get to show them all the lovely pictures the children had drawn of Howly!'

Jade sighed and counted off on her fingers. 'A school dog needs to be properly toilet-trained . . . We don't want children stepping in dog mess. He seemed terrified of people . . . A school dog needs to be confident and professional . . .'

Eddie looked down at Howly, who was lying on the canteen floor with his head in his paws. This was the worst possible news – so why was Jade smiling?

'Anyway,' Jade was saying with a twinkle in her eye, 'the school board letter said they were happy for Howly to remain in school . . . as long as there was an adult whose sole job was to look after him! Someone to clear up any messes, and take him to training classes and teach him how to be a reading assistance dog.'

Eddie looked at Jade expectantly.

'So Mr Jarvis asked *me* if I'd like the job of being Howly's handler,' she grinned.

'*And you said yes!*' squealed Eddie.

Howly jumped up at Eddie's excited voice and then dived under the table, reappearing a moment later with a fork.

'Of course I did!' Jade laughed, and Eddie threw her arms round her.

'So he can stay? Howly can be our school dog?' she asked excitedly.

'Probably,' Jade said, and Eddie paused. 'The school board told Mr Jarvis they wanted Howly to go to dog-training classes and have a handler with him at all times when he's doing his reading job. But they also said they would review the situation and make their final decision in the summer.'

'Oh,' said Eddie, biting her lip. What if the school board decided Howly couldn't be their reading assistance dog? 'What will he have to do at dog-training classes?' She thought it was funny that Howly would be going to school now.

'Well, some things he can already do – like *sit, down, stay* and *come* when he's called,' Jade told her.

Eddie nodded.

'He'll need to allow himself to be brushed – and let someone examine his paws, ears and teeth.'

'Howly loves being stroked,' Eddie smiled.

'And he loves being groomed too,' Jade smiled back.

Howly wagged his tail as she stroked him and then rolled over on his back for a tummy rub.

'The animal rescue centre is running its first dog-training course on Saturday mornings – starting this Saturday. Would you like to come along to Howly's classes with me?' Jade asked.

'Oh, yes, please,' Eddie said. If Howly did well in his classes and started properly listening to children read, then surely the school board would be pleased and let him stay.

'Has Jade shown you her surprise yet?' Coral asked Eddie as she came into the kitchen.

Eddie shook her head and looked questioningly at her friend.

'It's not just *my* surprise, Auntie Coral,' Jade said. 'You helped too and so did little Howly.'

'What is it?' Eddie asked.

Coral beckoned to her and she followed Jade and her aunt down the corridor to the library.

'Oh!'

There was a small storage room next to the library that Eddie had never given much thought to before. But now she couldn't miss it – there was a huge photograph of Howly on the door, and WELCOME TO HOWLY'S READING ROOM written in big letters underneath. Jade opened the door and Eddie went inside. There were two comfy beanbags, a water bowl for Howly and more pictures of him on the walls. Some of them were photographs, but lots were the paintings and drawings that the children had done.

Eddie gazed around in wonder. There was a colourful rug on the floor, and along the side of the room was a shelf absolutely bursting with books.

'It's beautiful!' Eddie said, while Howly went to sniff at something very interesting – a glass jar full of dog biscuits in the corner. 'Can I give him one?' Eddie asked.

'Of course,' Jade said, 'but get him to sit first! Howly's been practising.'

'He's a very clever little puppy,' Coral said with a smile.

But Eddie knew that already.

'*Sit*, Howly,' she commanded.

Howly immediately sat down and put his paw out to her. Delighted, Eddie rewarded him with a biscuit shaped like a bone.

Chapter 12

For the rest of the week Eddie helped Mr Jones plant seeds in the garden and worked with Jade and Coral to finish setting up Howly's reading room.

And Howly needed to practise being a reading dog. So Eddie sat down on one beanbag, with Howly snuggled up next to her, and read to him from Mrs Parks's book.

While Eddie read, she stroked Howly. He stayed very calm and sometimes looked up at her when she was reading. It was a wonderful feeling.

When she'd finished, she reached into his jar and gave him one of Mrs Hulu's sweet potato biscuits to say *Thank you for listening to me read*. Howly thought sweet potato biscuits were very fine indeed.

There were even more treats on Saturday when he went to his first training class at the animal rescue centre. Before the class, the instructor let the dogs have a play together, so Howly played chase with a spaniel and a boxer, wrestled with a Rottweiler and gave a tiny dog a lick.

When it was time for the class to begin properly, Eddie held his lead as the instructor told them what to do. Jade watched intently from the sidelines.

'*Sit*.'

Howly sat, but some of the other dogs didn't.

'Good puppy, Howly,' Eddie told him, giving him a peanut butter treat.

'*Stay*,' Eddie said, walking a few steps away. But Howly didn't want to be apart from her. He followed her at once.

'*Stay*'s always the difficult one,' the instructor told Eddie and Jade. 'But if you practise at home, he'll learn even more quickly.'

On Monday morning Howly started his job in his special reading room.

'I brought a book about a dog to read to Howly,' Abby told Jade as she sat down on the beanbag and Howly immediately joined her, just as he'd done with Eddie.

'Oh, he'll like that!' Jade said.

Miss Rodriguez had advised Jade that some children might feel nervous to read in front of her, so instead of joining them on the beanbags Jade busied herself nearby.

While Howly was listening to children read in his special room, Eddie was listening to Miss Rodriguez reading from Rosa Parks's book.

'Don't forget to make notes about which scenes you'd like to include in the play for Juneteenth,' the teacher told Eddie's class as she turned to the next page.

' "When the Ku Klux Klan came to their neighbourhood. Rosa's grandfather stayed up all night with a rifle next to him just in case – and Rosa slept right beside his chair. Luckily the Ku Klux Klan never came to her grandfather's house." '

'We definitely should include that bit,' Josh said. 'Can I play Rosa's grandfather?'

But no one looked very enthusiastic about wearing the Ku Klux Klan's long robes and pointed hat.

'I don't even want to pretend that I'm one of them.'

'We could make them puppets or scarecrows like we're going to do for the mean bus driver,' Eddie said. 'They could be papier mâché.'

'Good idea,' said Miss Rodriguez. 'We'll need lots of newspapers so if you have any at home, you could bring them in.'

'When did the Ku Klux Klan start?' Livvy asked Miss Rodriguez.

'It's been going since the time of the Civil War,' the teacher told her.

'More than a hundred years!' said Joshua.

'Hope it doesn't last for much longer!' said Robin.

'Are children in the Ku Klux Klan too?' Eddie asked.

'Oh, I hope not!' said Miss Rodriguez.

'Why do the KKK hate us? We haven't done anything to them!' Harry said.

Miss Rodriguez shook her head sadly. 'I know, Harry.' She turned back to the book. '"Rosa had to leave school early because her mother and grandmother were sick and she had to look after them."'

The children clamoured to play Rosa's family, and Miss Rodriguez smiled.

'Did you know Rosa got married when she was nineteen? To a man named Raymond Parks.'

'We have to include the wedding!' said Matilda. 'I love weddings – can I be a bridesmaid?'

'Did Rosa Parks have bridesmaids at her wedding to Raymond?'

'I'm not sure . . .'

'It would be nice to have some.'

'Then let's.'

'I hope you're good at changing clothes fast, Eddie – because there're going to be a lot of costume changes!' Livvy said. 'I'm very good at getting changed quickly,' she added pointedly.

Eddie wished she'd stop going on about it. It was making her even more nervous.

'Rosa's spent her whole life trying to help people,' Miss Rodriguez said. 'And this is what she wrote, "Everyone living in peace and harmony and love . . . that's the goal that we seek."'

When Miss Rodriguez read those words, Eddie looked up from her notebook.

'I think I should say that in the play,' she said boldly and Miss Rodriguez smiled.

'Good idea.'

'Civil rights are about everyone working towards a better tomorrow. Like the Universal Declaration of Human Rights,' Harry said, looking at the poster pinned to the wall that listed the thirty rights that all humans should have.

Miss Rodriguez nodded.

'It was signed by forty-eight countries, including America, in 1948. It states that all human beings are born free and equal,' she said.

'Is there a Declaration of Animal Rights too?' Eddie asked. 'I think Howly would probably say all animals should be treated kindly and have lots of love and cuddles if they want them. And play time too. *And* tasty food!' She thought of him in his reading room, getting treats for listening to the children read, and smiled to herself.

When the bell rang for the end of the day, Howly's ears pricked up. As soon as Jade opened the door to his reading room, he raced down the corridor, back into Eddie's class and straight over to her, his tail wagging excitedly.

Jade followed him, laughing, and told Eddie that he'd listened to two Second Graders read, one after the other, and both of them had brought dog stories.

'I just want the reading sessions to be a happy, productive time for everyone,' Jade told Eddie as they left the school building and headed home across the park. As they passed the trash can by the wall, Eddie thought about how she had found the puppy. She felt a warm, grateful glow at Jade's words – there could be no better job for a dog who loved children as much as little Howly.

Chapter 13

Every day when Howly arrived at the school, his breakfast of scrambled eggs was waiting for him. After that, he played with Eddie and her friends for a few minutes in the schoolyard before heading to his reading room with Jade. But one morning, a few weeks after the routine had started, something changed.

'Today we're going on a trip,' Eddie told Howly, as she clipped his lead to his collar.

She led him towards the big yellow school bus, but then felt a tug on the lead. When she looked round, she saw that Howly had stopped dead, staring at the bus. Eddie frowned and watched him carefully, but a moment later he shook himself all over, and headed over to her. Eddie thought how he'd grown since those first days after she'd found him.

When they reached the door of the bus, none other than Mrs Parks herself was standing there. Howly wagged his tail and they joined the queue of children waiting and chatting excitedly.

'Good morning, Eddie; welcome, Howly,' Mrs Parks said as they climbed aboard.

Howly bounded up the steps and when Eddie sat down at a window seat near the front, he hopped on to the seat next to her.

'Oh, Howly, there's not enough room for me too if you sit there!' Livvy said, coming to join them. Howly moved over to sit on Eddie's lap instead.

Once everyone was seated, Miss Rodriguez handed out packed lunches made by Mrs Hulu – sandwiches, cookies and an apple for everyone.

'This one's for Howly,' Miss Rodriguez said to Eddie, and she gave her a bag of sweet potato dog treats.

'I'll look after yours for you, Howly,' Eddie said, as she popped his treats into her backpack.

'Today we're going to the Detroit River,' Mrs Parks told them from the front of the bus. 'Where escaped slaves made their bid for freedom.'

Mr Jones drove the yellow school bus and Howly sat on Eddie's lap, looking out of the window. They all waved to Officer Baines when they saw him ride past on his bicycle, and he waved back.

'I see the Motown Museum,' Livvy said, pointing excitedly.

'Oh, I've been to that museum too – *Hitsville USA*!' said Harry, from the other side of the bus.

'The Motown stars were so glamorous,' Matilda said from the seat behind. 'Especially Diana Ross and the Supremes.'

It took forty minutes to get to the huge river and Howly spent most of the journey looking out of the window – and sometimes at Eddie's backpack where he knew his treats were. Eddie remembered how he'd been sick in the car with Mr Jarvis, and kept a careful eye on him. He didn't look sick at all, though.

Mr Jones parked the school bus near the Detroit to Canada tunnel. As the children got off, Howly sniffed the unfamiliar air and the interesting river smell.

A gull screeched as it flew overhead, and Howly cowered.

'Don't worry, puppy, we won't let him hurt you,' said Harry.

Howly went to sniff at a bit of burger someone had dropped, but a gull swooped down before he got the chance. Howly tried to chase after the bird and yapped in protest as it flew off.

'That gull was fast!' Eddie said.

Howly looked up at her and then back at the gull and gave a whine.

Then Mrs Parks started talking and everyone went quiet.

'Detroit was very important to runaway slaves because of the river. At its narrowest, it's only half a mile wide . . .'

'I can swim half a mile,' said Joshua. 'It's thirty-three laps of the swimming pool.'

Mrs Parks nodded. 'And so could some slaves – although swimming in a river would be much harder than swimming laps in a pool.'

'Yes, because of the currents . . .'

'And the tides . . .'

'You could get swept away . . .'

'Or drowned . . .'

'Or caught by a slave catcher . . .'

'Or saved by someone from the Underground Railroad in a boat,' said Miss Rodriguez.

Mrs Parks nodded. 'Yes. Half of the Detroit River is in the USA and the other half's in Canada. The centre of the river is where the two countries meet. Once the fugitive slaves were in Canada, they were safe, so as you can see, Detroit was a very important place back then.'

They all followed Mrs Parks to a large boat that was waiting on a jetty.

'Shall we climb on board?' Mrs Parks asked the children.

'Yes!'

'I've never been on a boat trip before,' said Robin.

Howly kept close to Eddie as they walked along the wooden pier to the boat.

A tour guide wearing a captain's hat gave all the children and grown-ups lifejackets to wear, but there wasn't a dog equivalent for Howly.

'Don't worry, I'll look after you,' Eddie told him.

'Me too,' said Harry, sitting down next to them.

Howly pressed himself close to Eddie when the motor started up, but once they were off he sat by Eddie's feet and looked around.

'Imagine you were an escaped slave looking across the river from Detroit towards Canada – and freedom,' the tour guide said into a microphone so that everyone could hear.

'There should be a statue so no one forgets what happened here,' Eddie said.

Mrs Parks overheard her. 'Maybe one day there will be,' she smiled. 'I hope so. I think there should be one statue here and another in Canada across the river, welcoming the newly freed people to their new lives. It's thought that thirty thousand ex-slaves settled in Canada.'

'Some escaped slaves came through Texas to Mexico,' Miss Rodriguez told the children. 'And Mexican people tried their best to hide them – even when the Texas Rangers came looking for them.'

'Some Native Americans helped the slaves too, or so I've heard,' said Mr Jones.

'And sometimes slaves used to escape to Native American reservations and live there. I'm part Native American on my mother's side,' Mrs Parks said.

'Me too!' said Jack excitedly. 'My gran's Native American.'

As the boat chugged along, they learnt about the famous Harriet Tubman, an escaped slave who helped many others to escape via the Underground Railroad – all the while carrying a bounty on her head.

'What's a bounty?' Harry asked.

'A money reward for the person who captured her,' Livvy told him.

'Would Harriet Tubman have been killed if she was caught?' Josh asked.

'Probably – she certainly wouldn't have been shown any mercy,' Mrs Parks told him. 'They used bloodhounds to track people.'

'Bloodhounds have been used for tracking since the middle ages,' Eddie said, proud to contribute. She'd read about it during her research on dogs in the First World War.

Howly looked through the rails at the waves the boat was making. He kept close to Eddie.

'Harriet Tubman must have been one brave lady, Eddie said thoughtfully.

Mrs Parks nodded. 'Yes she was. She led many slaves to freedom and she did it all despite suffering severe epileptic seizures brought on by a cruel slave master when she was a child. She died in 1913 – the year I was born. John Brown, the famous abolitionist, called her General Tubman.'

Eddie looked down at Howly on her lap and hid a smile as Harry nudged her. Mrs Parks hadn't heard the puppy howling along to 'John Brown's Body', but Eddie was sure she'd love it.

'What I want to know is how could an underground railroad be kept secret? Trains so are noisy – and big!' Harry said.

'I love trains,' said Robin, who was sitting on Harry's other side. 'Did you know that loads of people were brought over from China to help build the first Transcontinental Railroad back in 1863? It stretched for almost two thousand miles!'

'The Chinese immigrants suffered terrible racism too,' Miss Rodriguez said, shaking her head.

'Actually, the Underground Railroad wasn't a real railway, Harry,' Mrs Parks said. 'It was a secret network of people helping escaped slaves to freedom. It was just called the Underground Railroad to confuse people.'

'There's thought to have been over two hundred Underground Railroad stops – and the Detroit River was the final one before freedom,' the tour guide told them. 'The codename for travelling to Detroit was "Freedom Unlimited" or "Midnight Express". His microphone was a bit squeaky and Howly looked quizzically at him every time he spoke. Eddie wondered if he thought the guide was a giant squeaking mouse and that made her laugh so much she had to put her hand over her mouth so no one would think she was being rude.

'People waited over on the other side of the river in Windsor, Canada, to greet the often overwhelmed slaves.'

Eddie stared at the wide, deep Detroit River and tried to imagine herself as an escaped slave making her way to freedom. She looked at little Howly who had his head to one side and was staring at the man with the microphone or maybe he was staring at the microphone waiting for it to squeak.

'I'd have taken you with me, Howly,' she said.

He looked up at her and gave a yap and wagged his tail as if he knew exactly what she was talking about.

'White people are just nasty and mean,' Livvy said.

'Well, Livvy, many white people have actually tried to help our cause over the years and are still doing so,' said Mrs Parks gently.

She pointed to the banks of the river. 'Seymour Finney was one of them. He had a stable where he hid escaped slaves before they went off to Canada – and a hotel where he got slave catchers drunk so they couldn't catch a fly!'

'But why are so many of them mean?' Harry said.

'It's a way to keep us downtrodden and I think it's because they're ashamed,' Mrs Parks said. 'Ashamed of what their race did to ours for so long.'

'You mean making black people their slaves?'

Mrs Parks nodded. 'I hate to think about how many hundreds of thousands of people suffered because of it. That's why we should always celebrate Juneteenth, the day the last enslaved African Americans in the USA were finally freed.'

'It's terrible,' Harry said. 'How could people be so cruel?'

Eddie felt the same.

'Slavery was a worldwide trade,' Miss Rodriguez said. 'Not just in America and not just black people. Even at the start of the nineteenth century, nearly three-quarters of *all* people were trapped as slaves or unpaid servents working off a debt.'

'Are there still slaves today?' Eddie asked.

Miss Rodriguez exchanged a look with Mrs Parks. 'Not in America legally, no. Not since the thirteenth amendment to the US Constitution back in 1865. But there are still many unfortunate people trapped as slaves throughout the world.'

'But what about the declaration of human rights that's on our classroom wall. It says "*All humans are born free and equal in dignity and rights.*" ' Eddie said.

'Shouldn't that protect people?' Robin asked.

'It certainly helps,' Mrs Parks told him. 'Although it's not a legally binding document.

And people like Gary Tyler, a teenager who was wrongfully arrested back in 1974, and still in prison despite rallies and protests by human rights activists, show that it doesn't always. Although I do so hope one day he'll be free and will do everything in my power to help him.'

'Why didn't the slaves try to escape? Why did they just put up with being treated like that?' Livvy asked Mrs Parks. '*I* wouldn't have.'

Mrs Parks pressed her lips together. 'First of all, they *did* try to escape and lots of them died in the attempt. But if you tried to escape and were caught, dreadful things happened. You might have your foot cut off, you might be locked underground in a box for weeks . . . or worse.' Mrs Parks sighed. 'If only people spent as much time thinking of how they could help others instead of hurt them – well, the world would be a much better place for everyone: people, animals and the environment.'

'Is there any hope at all, Mrs Parks? Sometimes it seems like so many bad things happen,' Eddie said.

'Oh yes, lots and lots of hope, my dears,' Mrs Parks replied, sounding surprised at the question.

'But where?' Livvy said.

'Why, I'm looking right at it. *You* are the hope, my dears, the hope of the future lies with the children of today. If one woman refusing to give up her seat on a bus can make as much difference as it did then, just think of what you could achieve and what could happen if you really set your mind to it!'

The boat reached Belle Isle in the centre of the river.

'Belle Isle Zoo's just opened again,' the tour guide told them.

Eddie had never been to the theme park island, although she thought she'd like to visit it very much one day. The tour boat sailed under the bridge.

'One day soon I hope to see a world where people from every race and religion work together to improve life for everyone,' Mrs Parks said and she smiled her twinkling-eyed smile.

When they got off the boat, Howly sniffed at Eddie's backpack. He was getting hungry and looked up at Eddie hopefully.

'Hatred is a choice you make,' Mrs Parks continued, as she led them to a grassy park area with benches to eat their lunch. 'You can always choose to be kind and loving instead.'

Eddie nodded, as she pulled off her backpack and rummaged around for a notebook and pen. She thought that Mrs Parks's words would be good to include in the play too.

Howly tried to stuff his head into her backpack. Food at last!

'One minute – let me get the treats out,' Eddie said, grinning.

Howly sat down and extended his paw towards her, then Eddie gave him one of his sweet potato treats.

'Gone in a nanosecond,' Joshua laughed, as Howly gulped it down and then looked up at Eddie for more.

Chapter 14

Once Eddie had finished eating her sandwiches, helped by Howly, who'd eaten his treats in no time at all, she took him for a walk across the grass. Through the trees she saw a vast round building with lots of windows.

'What's that?' Eddie asked Mrs Parks, who was sharing her sandwiches with Mr Jones. Howly thought the sandwiches looked very interesting. He sat down and held out his paw.

'That's Cobo Hall Arena – where the Detroit Walk to Freedom march of 1963 ended,' Mrs Parks said.

'The march where we first met,' smiled Mr Jones.

'And you gave me your umbrella,' Mrs Parks chuckled.

'That building is where Reverend King first gave what was to become his famous "I Have a Dream" speech a few weeks later,' Mr Jones told Eddie and the other children.

'But why did the Walk to Freedom march happen?' asked Livvy.

'Well, among other things, we were protesting against inequality in hiring and wages, education and housing,' Mrs Parks said. 'And the marching did make a difference, I feel, although we still have sad examples of discrimination like the wall in your playground.'

'Why do you keep calling it a segregation wall when it's not segregating anything?' asked Joshua immediately.

Mrs Parks sighed. 'The truth is that the wall in your schoolyard, and the park and beyond, was built way back in 1941 by a white developer who wanted to build new houses for white people near the black neighbourhood that already existed. But he couldn't get the money to do so from the Federal Housing Association until he built a wall separating the two neighbourhoods. So he got his men to put up the wall. It was built during the time when folks weren't allowed to mix. Things are better now, much better than they were when we had the Freedom March back in 1963.'

'Were people hurt on the march?' Eddie asked Mrs Parks.

The older lady shook her head. 'Although there were hundreds of thousands of marchers, no one was killed or injured and no arrests were made. It was a peaceful protest, but one that needed to be made if we were ever to have equality in this country.'

'How long did the march take?' Joshua wanted to know.

'Well, it started on Woodward Avenue and Adelaide, continued on Woodward on to Jefferson, and concluded at Cobo Hall Arena. So, about half an hour if you walk at a regular pace, and a bit quicker if you speed along,' Mr Jones told him.

'Could *we* do the march?' Eddie said suddenly, struck with an idea. 'Follow the route you took.'

Mr Jones and Mrs Parks looked at each other.

'We've got time if you'd like to,' Miss Rodriguez said, and Eddie knew her teacher wanted to take part in the march too.

'I could drive the bus up to Woodward Avenue and Adelaide, drop you and the children off, and then meet you halfway, if you like?' Mr Jones said.

This time the journey was very short indeed.

'Here we are,' Mr Jones said, as everyone got off the bus.

Howly looked up at Eddie and wagged his tail.

'First we head down Woodward,' Mrs Parks said, and everyone followed her down the wide street with houses that were much grander than where Eddie lived.

Eddie tried to imagine thousands of African Americans marching together, determined to bring about change for the better.

Howly sniffed at everything as they passed.

The houses soon gave way to tall office buildings and Eddie thought how the crowds of people must have stopped the traffic. There would have been so many of them that cars and buses wouldn't have been able to get through.

Howly marched along beside her.

Harry started whistling 'John Brown's Body' and Howly looked up at him with his head on one side. But the puppy seemed so intent on marching that he didn't join in with the usual howl. Even when some of the other children started whistling too, Howly still didn't join in. Eddie hadn't been able to whistle since she'd got her adult teeth, but the tuneful melody did make her smile as they marched along.

Mr Jones joined them from the other direction when they reached Jefferson, and soon they'd all stopped outside the round building Eddie had seen through the trees.

'Even though Cobo Hall Arena's huge, it still wasn't big enough to fit everyone in. Lots of us listened to the activists' speeches from outside,' Mr Jones said.

'Motown Records recorded Martin Luther King's famous speech. Did you know that he didn't keep any of the money from that recording? He said it should all go towards furthering the civil rights cause,' Mrs Parks said.

'Time we were heading back, I think,' Miss Rodriguez said, looking at her watch.

'I parked near the City-County Building,' Mr Jones said, pointing towards a massively tall construction with a giant green statue in front of it.

Eddie's mouth fell open. Before her was the famous green Spirit of Detroit statue. In one hand the massive cross-legged sculpture held golden rays, and in the other he had a small golden family of people.

'It's beautiful,' Eddie gasped. She'd seen pictures of it before, but it was impossible to grasp how imposing and magnificent it was until you stood in front of it. Behind the statue, the City-County Building stretched up into the blue sky towards the clouds.

Howly had had a very busy day and was tired. He sat down next to Eddie's foot, but the next moment spotted a cat running into the building, and his energy returned. In a second he'd slipped his lead and was up the steps and yapping as he chased after it.

'No! Howly, come back!' Eddie cried, and she went running up the steps and into the building after him.

The cat went down one corridor and up another and Howly chased, completely oblivious to Eddie's calls.

'Howly!' Eddie shouted as she ran after him. 'Howly, come back!' He could run very fast when he wanted to and she was frightened that she'd lose him. *Howly!*

She'd almost caught up with them when the cat and the puppy ran in through an open glass door.

Eddie tumbled in after them. The cat jumped up on to a desk, then on to a lamp and up on to the top of a cupboard. Howly stared up at it.

'Got you!' Eddie gasped, grabbing his collar and putting his lead back on.

The cat stared down at Howly from the top of the cupboard and gave a *miaow*. Howly wagged his tail.

Eddie slowly realized the room was full of official-looking people – people who were staring at the commotion her puppy had caused. She felt her face burning red.

'I'm very sorry,' she said. 'I didn't mean . . . sorry.'

'He is a lovely little puppy,' said a lady, standing up from her desk and coming over to give Howly a stroke. The cat looked down at the dog and gave a flick of its tail.

'Thanks,' said Eddie nervously. 'Er – which way's the exit?'

'This way,' the lady said kindly, as they went down one corridor and up another. As they walked, Howly sniffed around and Eddie told the lady about their school trip. When she said they had Rosa Parks with them – *the* Rosa Parks – the lady became very excited indeed.

'Come on,' said Eddie, 'I'll introduce you!'

When they rejoined the rest of the school party, Mrs Parks shook the lady's hand.

'My name is Sofia Matthews,' the lady said. 'It's so lovely to meet you. Such an honour!'

'Mrs Parks has been telling us about the segregation wall that goes through our playground,' Livvy said. 'We don't want it there.'

'Oh – oh dear,' said Sofia Matthews. 'Are you from Birwood Elementary? Are you talking about the Birwood Wall? I'm from the Planning and Development Department, and I'm afraid to tell you it can't be taken down. Much as I wish that it could!'

Then Eddie had an idea. She whispered it to Miss Rodriguez, who motioned her to ask Sofia Matthews. Eddie did so, feeling nervous all over again.

'What an interesting idea! Wait just one minute and I'll check,' Sofia said, hurrying back inside the building.

She returned a few minutes later. 'The wall must remain, as I said, but we can grant you permission to paint it,' she said.

'Brilliant!' said Eddie.

Howly wagged his tail, as Sofia gave him another stroke.

'Time we were getting back to school,' Miss Rodriguez said to the class. 'Your parents will be worried if we're late.'

Howly was so tired by now that Eddie had to help him up the steps of the bus. It had been a very long day with lots of exciting things to hear and see and smell – and chase.

'You have a nice sleep, little marching puppy,' Eddie said as he curled up half on her lap, half on the seat and started to snore softly. Livvy went to sit next to Chloe instead as there wasn't much room for her too.

'If it hadn't been for you, Howly, we wouldn't have met Sofia Matthews and got permission for my idea!' Eddie smiled. She watched him sleeping, already thinking of her plan to turn the concrete wall into something beautiful.

Chapter 15

When Eddie's mum and dad came home from work, they brought pizza with them. She expected them to be tired, as usual, but they were almost bursting with excitement.

'You'll never guess what's happened, Eddie!' said her mum, as Eddie opened the pizza box.

'Mm-mm!'

'Nelson Mandela is coming to Detroit! And he's going to visit our car factory!' said Dad.

Eddie almost dropped her slice of pizza in surprise. 'He's coming here?'

Her dad nodded. 'He wants to thank the United Automobile Workers and its members for never giving up on asking for his freedom and pushing for him to be released from prison.'

'He's coming to *our* car factory and *we'll get to see him*!' Her mum grinned round a mouthful of pizza. 'Now tell us about your school outing.'

Eddie told them about the boat trip and how they'd followed the route of the march that Mrs Parks and Mr Jones had gone on in 1963. Then she told them about Howly running into the office building and the lady that they'd met.

'Mrs Parks used to help African Americans with their housing,' said Eddie. 'She told us all about the segregation wall in the park and playground –'

'The *what*?' Dad said in disbelief.

'You mean that wall in your school playground?' said Mum.

'And the park,' Eddie said.

'That's terrible!'

'What a horrible reminder of the past,' said her dad.

'Should be torn down.'

'Pulled apart brick by brick.'

'The Planning and Development Department said we can't do that when I asked them – but I had a better idea,' Eddie said. 'To turn that ugly old concrete into something colourful and amazing.'

Dad grinned at her and then turned to Eddie's mum. 'Do you know, we've got one smart daughter,' he said.

'Yes, I did,' said Mum. 'She takes after me.'

'Oh no, she definitely takes after me,' Dad laughed, as Eddie shook her head and beamed at them both.

'My dad might be able to get us some paint for the wall,' Eddie told Miss Rodriguez the next morning. 'He paints cars at the Ford factory. Nelson Mandela's going to be visiting their factory soon and my mum and dad are really excited about it!'

'This could all be part of our school's celebration of Nelson Mandela's visit to Detroit,' Miss Rodriguez said.

Mr Jarvis also thought Eddie's idea was an excellent one, and sent a letter home with the children to tell their parents about the school's new project.

Eddie's mum and dad told their friends at the car factory too, and everyone they spoke to wanted to help change it into a celebration wall instead of a segregation one.

Chapter 16

Every chance they got, Eddie and her class worked on transforming the wall. The rest of the school and lots of the parents and community volunteers joined in too. Soon, Eddie's vision started to take place – what was once a bland grey wall was being turned into a beautiful mural, with flowers and rainbows and butterflies everywhere. Eddie painted a picture of Howly running and then another one of him sitting down. She chuckled as she spotted a line of colourful paw prints along the side of the wall, courtesy of Howly when he'd stepped in a tray full of paint and then chased after a ball.

'I think I like his little paw prints best of all,' Eddie's mum laughed when she saw them. Howly looked up at her with his head to one side and wagged his tail.

Eddie's dad gave him a tentative stroke. 'He sure is a sweet little pup.'

Mr Jarvis said it was fine for the children to add their handprints too – so everyone did.

'We should add pictures of famous people like Mrs Parks,' Robin said.

'And Oprah Winfrey and Maya Angelou . . .'

'Mrs Parks could be boarding the bus in Montgomery . . .' said Reece.

'Don't forget Harry Belafonte – I'm named after him!' said Harry.

'And we could add other bus protestors – like the ones in our play,' Livvy suggested.

'The wall can be a celebration of all our great heroes!' Eddie said. Howly wagged his tail. Eddie knew he liked the sound of her voice, especially when she was excited.

'Martin Luther King and Harriet Tubman . . .'

'Mister Mandela, and Muhammad Ali, and Malcolm X . . .'

'Plus our families and friends . . .'

'Everyone who's important to us . . .'

'Like you, Howly,' Robin told the puppy, who gave a happy howl.

Eddie smiled as she started painting a picture of Grandma and Grandpa next to one she'd done of Howly. She practised her lines for the Rosa Parks play in her head as she painted.

'There are so many amazing people and animals – we might not be able to fit them all on this bit of the wall,' Miss Rodriguez said.

'Then we'll just have to paint the rest of the wall too!' Eddie said. 'And there're two sides of it, remember. It stretches for half a mile in total. That's a lot of painting!'

It didn't take long for them to run out of paint. Eddie wondered if there was a quick way to raise more money. She gazed up at the bright blue sky, wiping a bead of sweat from her forehead.

'Let's sell lemonade outside the school!' Eddie said. 'There's a recipe for it in my Edna Lewis cookbook.'

'Good idea!'

On Saturday morning Howly went to his final canine class with Eddie and Jade. Next time they went it would be for his exam.

'He's done very well and I'm very pleased with him,' the instructor said.

*

In the afternoon, the weather was as fine as could be, and Eddie and Harry set up a table outside the school. They had sold four glasses of lemonade and everyone who'd bought one had said it was delicious. They were in the process of mixing some more sugar into the jug when a police car drove up and screeched to a halt.

Eddie and Harry looked at each other. This policeman wasn't like Officer Baines. He didn't look friendly at all, just cross and hot. Eddie would have offered him a glass of lemonade if he hadn't been so grumpy. Howly wagged his tail, but the policeman scowled at him.

'There's been a complaint about this lemonade stand,' he said.

'Why?' Eddie gasped. They'd made the Edna Lewis recipe exactly as it said in the book and it tasted delicious. Why would anyone complain?

'We haven't done anything wrong,' said Harry. His voice shook a little.

'Do you have a licence to sell lemonade?' the policeman asked them.

Eddie shook her head. She didn't even know they'd needed one.

Officer Baines came cycling down the street.

'Hi, there,' he called out. 'Beautiful day.'

Howly ran over to him as soon as he stopped.

The other policeman looked over at Officer Baines and scowled again.

'Is something wrong?' Officer Baines asked him.

'They don't have a permit.'

Eddie couldn't take her eyes off the other policeman's gun on his hip. She and Harry looked at each other, frightened.

'Oh, that's all taken care of,' Officer Baines laughed. 'Don't you worry about that. I expect you've got some real criminals to catch.'

The other policeman didn't look amused. 'Yes, I have! I wish people driving past lemonade stands like this one didn't always think they have to call the police and report it. We've got *much* more important things to attend to.'

'Guess they've got nothing better to do,' Officer Baines said as the other officer headed back to his car. Just before he opened the driver's door, though, he looked over at Howly and frowned.

'Don't you know the Michigan Leash Law?' he said to Eddie.

Eddie shook her head, worried. She didn't know what he was talking about, but it sounded bad. She remembered the security guard at Macy's when she was visiting her grandparents.

This policeman was looking at her in the same way.

'And how old is he? Dogs over six months must be registered and wear a collar at all times. Otherwise it could be . . .'

Eddie didn't wait to hear what the policeman had to say next. Her head was so frightened and full of all the terrible things she'd discovered recently about the world that she turned and ran. Howly went chasing after her.

'Hey, you, come back!' she heard the policeman shout, but she didn't stop. She felt so frenzied that she half expected a bullet to come whizzing past her ear. She ran into the playground and through the swing doors of the school.

'Eddie!' Mr Jones said, as she and Howly raced past him.

She knew she had to find somewhere to hide. Somewhere the policeman wouldn't look for her. The cupboard where the mops were kept was open and she ran inside with Howly right behind her, and closed the door. She sank down on to the floor and pulled her knees up to her chest. It was dark in the cupboard and the puppy whined to be let out.

'Sssh,' Eddie said. The last thing she needed now was for Howly to howl and tell the policeman where they were. 'We'll be safe here,' she said, although she didn't really know if it was true. She hugged the little dog to her. 'I don't want him to take you away,' she said.

Outside in the corridor she could hear footsteps going up and down, and the murmur of voices. But the cupboard door didn't open and gradually Eddie's heart stopped beating at a million times a minute. Then, eventually, Howly curled up and went to sleep next to her.

Eddie waited for what felt like a long time after it had all gone quiet before she stood up.

She didn't want the policeman to take Howly to the dog pound – she might never see him again and she couldn't bear the thought of that.

Howly stood up and stretched, then looked at the door. It was only at that moment that Eddie realized there was no handle on the inside.

Chapter 17

Eddie banged on the door.

'Help, help! Isn't anyone out there?'

She hated the thought of being stuck in the cupboard and she knew Howly wouldn't last very long without needing to go potty. He was already walking around in anxious circles by her feet.

'He-elp!'

But still no one came. Eddie banged and banged on the door and finally sank back down. It looked like she and Howly would have to sleep there all night.

Eddie curled up tight and wrapped her arms round herself to try to keep warm. She felt grateful at least to be inside, thinking about the poor runaway slaves who would have had to find somewhere to sleep outside. Howly came and lay next to her and she hugged him.

Eddie felt so exhausted that she finally fell asleep, only for the door to swing open suddenly with a burst of bright afternoon light.

'*Eddie!*' Mr Jones said. 'At last we've found you.'

Office Baines and Harry were with him.

'You can't take Howly. Please don't take him,' Eddie begged her favourite policeman.

'Hush, hush now,' Officer Baines said. 'No one's taking Howly anywhere.'

A moment later, Eddie's mum and dad came running down the corridor.

'We've been looking everywhere . . .'

'Officer Baines came to our house . . .'

'I'm OK!' Eddie said, relief washing over her. 'And Howly's OK too.'

Howly looked up at them all and wagged his tail.

On 19 June, it was the opening performance. Eddie took a deep breath, just about to put on her first costume, when Miss Rodriguez told her that Mrs Parks would like to have a word. Eddie had been thrilled when the class discovered Mrs Parks would be attending the performance – it was exciting, but made her very nervous too.

'Yes, Mrs Parks?' Eddie said, when she found her over near the wall by a painting of Muhammad Ali. Next to him were paintings of Recy Taylor and Gertrude Perkins – two women whom Rosa Parks had campaigned to get justice for. Harry had painted the likenesses painstakingly over the last few weeks.

'Such a lovely man,' Mrs Parks said, touching the painting of Muhammad Ali. She turned. 'I've got something for you, Eddie.'

She opened the bag she was holding and pulled out what looked like a multicoloured piece of material.

'In all my years as a seamstress I'd never thought to make a dog coat before,' Mrs Parks said, 'but I thought little Howly deserved one!' She handed the material to Eddie. 'Although it's not as good as the one that Sergeant Stubby had made for him by the French ladies in the Second World War,' she smiled.

'It's beautiful,' Eddie said, as she traced her finger over the coat. Mrs Parks had covered it in pictures of medals. One of them said, HAPPY HOWLY, and another said, FOR LISTENING TO CHILDREN READ.

'Howly loves doing that,' Eddie said softly.

'I know,' said Mrs Parks. 'Miss Rodriguez told me that everyone's reading is improving by leaps and bounds because of it!'

Eddie looked back down at the coat. 'Thank you so much, Mrs Parks,' Eddie said, and before she could stop herself, she'd thrown her arms round the great lady.

Mrs Parks patted her on the back. 'You're very welcome,' she said. 'Oh, and, Eddie – my friends call me Rosa. You and Howly are definitely my friends. In fact, I think everyone at this school is! Now you'd better hurry and get changed. I'm looking forward to seeing the play.'

Eddie did as Rosa said. She'd practised and practised her lines, but was running through them one more time in front of the mirror when Livvy appeared by her side.

'Don't worry if you forget your lines,' she said. 'I'll tell you what they are. I learnt them all myself, just in case!'

Eddie knew Livvy was trying to be helpful, but it gave her a nervous flip in her stomach. She straightened her back, determined to play her part perfectly.

The audience hushed as the blackout curtains at the windows were pulled and the stage lights were turned on.

The first scene of the play was of Mrs Parks as a baby – although to Eddie's relief she didn't have to pretend to be a baby. The class had made a papier mâché head with a bonnet and wrapped it in blankets.

The second scene was of Rosa as a little girl at school. Abby, the First Grader whose reading had improved a whole lot since she'd been reciting to Howly, played the young Rosa, and again in the scene at her grandfather's house.

Everyone booed when the Ku Klux Klan puppets showed up, and cheered when Josh, wearing a fake beard, waved his rifle made from painted toilet rolls.

Eddie took a deep breath and smoothed down her costume. It was her turn now. She stepped out on stage wearing a wedding dress, with Harry playing her husband, Raymond. Robin acted the part of the vicar who married them and spoke the lines in a deep gravelly voice.

When they were writing the play, the children hadn't known whether or not Rosa had had confetti at her wedding, but they'd chopped up lots of coloured tissue paper into tiny pieces and now threw it over Eddie and Harry in celebration.

For the important bus scene, they'd made the yellow bus out of one sheet of cardboard and cut holes in it for windows. Livvy, Matilda and Jack stood behind some of the windows, playing various other people who had protested over bus segregation.

For this scene, Eddie wore an old-fashioned suit and a pair of glasses. As she boldly told the papier mâché bus driver that she refused to give up her seat, a bark sounded from the audience. She grinned, grateful for Howly's support down on Jade's lap.

During the bus boycott, everyone marched back and forth across the stage while the bus stood empty.

'No more bus segregation!' shouted Adam, dressed as a judge and holding a gavel.

The class and Eddie cheered. But the play wasn't over yet. Eddie and the rest of the children came back on stage holding placards representing all the different marches and causes that Mrs Parks had devoted her life to.

The play ended with the setting up of the Rosa and Raymond Parks Institute. Eddie also told the story of the Underground Railroad, and of the Freedom Riders of the 1960s – people of different races who'd sat together on buses in places where segregation was still going on.

Last of all Eddie said the words that she'd heard directly from Mrs Parks – 'Hatred is a choice you make. You can always choose to be kind and loving instead.'

She gazed out into the audience and was sure she saw Mrs Parks's eyes glistening as she smiled at Eddie.

At the end everyone came out on stage to take their bow. Eddie appeared last of all and everyone went mad with clapping and cheering. Her whole class, on stage with her, was applauding too. Officer Baines, who was in the second row, put two fingers in his mouth and gave a big whistle. Eddie's face felt very hot, but she couldn't stop smiling.

Howly jumped off Jade's lap and ran on to the stage to be with Eddie. She crouched down and hugged him as he gave her face a lick.

'Couldn't have played Rosa better myself,' Livvy told Eddie with a big grin, as they came off stage. 'You're a natural-born actress – just like me!'

'Thanks,' Eddie laughed, although she thought perhaps being the star of a play once in her life was enough for her.

Now it was almost time to sing 'John Brown's Body', so Eddie quickly put Howly's new coat on him.

'Don't you look smart?' she said, and Howly gave her face another quick lick.

'It's time!' Livvy hissed.

Still wearing her costume from the last scene, Eddie stood in the middle of the stage at the front. Howly was sitting next to her in his brand-new coat and the other children stood round them.

The class were looking at each other and smiling knowingly – they were well aware of what was going to happen once Howly heard them singing.

Miss Rodriguez started to play the music.

One of Howly's ears pricked up. Then he stood up and his tail began to wag. He opened his jaws, and as the children sang he howled along with delight.

They sang the song once standing still, and then again marching across the stage, with Howly trotting along behind Eddie. They kept on singing as they marched and Howly kept on howling, even when the singing and marching became faster and faster.

When the song was over, Eddie could see her mum, dad and grandparents cheering and hooting. The whole audience was standing up and clapping and shouting, 'Encore!'

Mr Jarvis came up on to the stage with Mrs Parks and another man that Eddie didn't recognize, who was wearing a grey suit.

'I'm sure we would all like to thank *everyone* from Miss Rodriguez's class for a most entertaining Juneteenth performance,' the headmaster said, and everyone started clapping and cheering again.

When it had finally quietened down, Mr Jarvis said, 'Birwood Elementary is honoured to have the lady who inspired this play with us today – Mrs Rosa Parks.'

And then there was yet more applause for the great lady.

Mrs Parks smiled. 'It's a pleasure to be here,' she said. 'I enjoyed the play for

Juneteenth – and the singing, howling and marching very much!'

'Would you do us the honour of presenting one of the performers with this certificate, Mrs Parks?' Mr Jarvis asked her, holding out an embossed piece of paper.

Mrs Parks nodded as she took it from him. 'This certificate is awarded by the American Kennel Club and is a Canine Good Citizen Award for Howly – and for Eddie and Jade, who took him along to the training classes.'

From her seat, Jade indicated that Eddie should take the certificate. So she and Howly stepped forward, Eddie shaking Mrs Parks's hand and Howly sitting down and putting his paw out to her.

'Well done, little dog,' she said, and Howly gently took the certificate in his mouth and looked up at Eddie.

'Yes – it's for you,' she told him with a smile.

'Mister Cartwright, from the school board, also has something to say,' Mr Jarvis announced. The man in the suit stepped forward.

'As you may know, we have been reviewing Howly's progress at Birwood Elementary over the last few months, and it is the school board's decision . . .'

Eddie held her breath and clenched her fists as she waited.

'. . . that Howly should be Birwood Elementary School's official Reading Assistance Dog.'

'You did it, Howly, you did it!' Eddie cried, barely hearing the clapping and cheering as she hugged him. A tear rolled down her face and Howly licked it up.

'I do have just one more request, Miss Rodriguez,' Mr Jarvis said.

'Yes?' Miss Rodriguez said, intrigued.

'Can we have "John Brown's Body" once more – and this time all of us will join in with the song.'

'Certainly,' Miss Rodriguez laughed.

Howly was over the moon when he heard the familiar tune again. He howled and howled.

Once the show was over, everyone headed out into the bright sunshine of the playground, where refreshments were waiting. Eddie's mum and dad were helping.

'You did so well, Eddie,' Grandma told her, as she gave Howly a stroke. 'And so did your little singing puppy.'

'We're very proud of you,' Grandpa said, bending down to give Howly a rub too. The little dog stretched up his neck so Grandpa could tickle underneath his chin.

'Blueberry cake?' Eddie's dad said, winking at Eddie as he offered her grandparents the plate of already cut cake.

'Mm-mm,' Eddie's grandma said as she took a slice and sampled it. 'This is delicious. Who made it?'

'Our very own budding little Edna Lewis,' Dad said as Eddie chuckled and took a piece too.

'Well done, Eddie,' said her grandad.

Howly looked at the cake in Eddie's hand and gave a whine.

'Here, puppy,' Mrs Hulu said, coming over with a smaller plate. 'I made some peanut butter cookies especially for you.'

Howly thought his cookie was very fine indeed. He ran over to a leaf that had blown in on the wind, picked it up and ran back to Mrs Hulu with it.

'Come and see the celebration wall, Grandma and Grandpa,' Eddie said. 'It looks amazing!'

'Oh yes – now the wall is a fine thing to see,' Mr Jones said, coming to join them. 'And the fruits and vegetables we've been growing round it are coming along wonderfully.'

'Once they're ready, we're going to eat them!' Eddie said.

Mrs Parks was looking at Robin's painting of Malcolm X on the wall. 'So full of conviction and pride. His spirit reminded me of my grandfather – unbowed and unbreakable,' she said.

'These are my grandparents,' Eddie told her, and they all shook hands. 'They're visiting for two whole weeks so we can all go to see Mr Mandela speaking at the Tiger Stadium on the 29th,' Eddie said. She was very pleased that her grandparents could stay for so long and really excited that she'd get to see Nelson Mandela.

'An unforgettable experience.' Mrs Parks smiled.

'It's such an honour to meet you, Mrs Parks,' Eddie's grandpa said.

'And an honour to meet you too. I recognize you from Eddie's painting,' Mrs Parks told them.

'What painting?' Eddie's grandparents asked in surprise, and Mrs Parks pointed further along the wall. 'What are we doing on there?'

'We don't believe it,' Eddie's grandparents said when they saw Eddie's painting of them on the wall too.

'We're celebrating the lives of everyone who's important to us, which is why there're lots of pictures of Howly. And you two are *very* important to me!' Eddie said, as her grandparents hugged her.

Mr Jarvis had also told the children to bring in pictures of their family, and people who were special to them, to add to the murals. Now there were so many photographs, drawings and paintings that they filled the whole wall where it crossed through the playground. Part of the school metal fence was covered too, and more pictures were coming all the time.

'One day I think the whole of that wall will be filled with colour and life. It wont be grey any more, but all the colours of the rainbow!' Eddie said.

Howly headed over to join two of his favourite people and see if they had any tasty food to spare.

Then Jade came out with a giant Japanese strawberry shortcake, closely followed by Mrs Hulu and Coral.

'This is the cake my mother made to celebrate our final release from the internment camp after the Second World War,' Mrs Hulu said, as Jade set the strawberry shortcake down on a table. 'I hope I've done as good a job as she did, though nothing could compare to the one she created! I can still remember the taste of it and I was only five years old at the time.'

As Mrs Hulu started to cut the magnificent cake Eddie looked at Jade. She seemed to be almost bursting with happiness.

'What is it?' Eddie asked her friend. From the look on Jade's face, it had to be more than just the prospect of eating cake.

'I've got a scholarship to Tuskegee Veterinary School,' she told Eddie, as Mrs Hulu put slices of cake on to paper plates and Coral passed them around. *I'm going to be a vet!* It's what I've always wanted, but I just didn't have the finances before. Mrs Parks had a word and the university has scholarships of its own. I applied and have been awarded one of them. I can hardly believe it – I feel like if I pinch myself I'll find out it's all a dream!'

'Such wonderful news,' said Coral, hugging her niece.

'I was wondering if you'd like to take on Jade's job of looking after our reading dog?' Mr Jarvis asked her, between mouthfuls of cake.

'Oh, I would!' Coral said.

'I'm so happy for you,' Eddie told Jade. 'You deserve it. You'll be a wonderful vet, won't she, Howly?'

The little dog wagged his tail and gave a yap, and then ran back to his new friends, who'd been very generous with tasty bits of food.

'It's hard to believe he's the same puppy that we saw before,' the man from the school board said. 'I can see why everyone loves him.'

Eddie frowned. What was going to happen to Howly in the evenings and overnight and at weekends now that Jade was leaving for Tuskegee, almost 900 miles away? Would Mr Jones be able to look after him? Or perhaps Mrs Hulu or Coral?

'Oh, Eddie, your mother and I have been thinking about little Howly,' Dad called out to her.

When she turned round, she saw to her surprise that Howly was sitting on her dad's lap.

'Do you think you'd be able to look after Howly properly and responsibly if he came to stay with us for the summer holidays?'

Eddie's mum was smiling. Howly jumped off her dad's lap and ran towards Eddie, as she bounded over to her parents and threw her arms round them.

'*Yes!* Thank you, thank you, thank you!' she said, as Howly jumped up and tried to join in.

'We'll see how we all get on together over the summer holiday, and if that works out . . . well . . .'

'Maybe he can stay with us forever?' Eddie said hopefully.

Her parents smiled. 'Maybe.'

'But you'll still bring him into school to be our reading dog next term, won't you?' Mr Jarvis said.

'Birwood Elementary wouldn't be the same without its school dog,' smiled Mrs Parks.

'I'll bring him,' Eddie promised.

Howly looked up at Eddie and wagged his tail.

Glossary

Apartheid: a system of government that existed in South Africa from 1948 until the early 1990s, while the country was governed by a white minority. People of different races were forced to live apart and the rights of many black people were restricted. The word 'apartheid' means 'separateness' in Afrikaans.

Children's March, the: a demonstration that took place in May 1963, when hundreds of African-American children in Birmingham, Alabama, walked out of school to protest peacefully against the inequalities in their city. Things turned ugly, however, when police sprayed the youngsters with powerful fire hoses, hit them with batons and used police dogs to frighten them.

***Croix de Guerre*, the:** first created in 1915, this is a military medal awarded by the French government for acts of bravery in conflict.

Detroit River, the: in the nineteenth century, thousands of slaves escaped from Detroit, Michigan, travelling a mile across this river into Canada, where slavery was against the law and they could live freely.

Edna Regina Lewis (13 April 1916–13 February 2006): a famous African-American chef, teacher and author, who raised the profile of Southern cooking, with the emphasis on fresh and locally grown ingredients.

Gary Tyler (July 1958–): aged sixteen, Gary Tyler was wrongfully convicted for the 1974 shooting of a white high-school student on a bus. He was sentenced to death at first by an all-white jury. Following his unfair trail, Rosa Parks campaigned relentlessly, speaking at a rally and meetings to get Tyler's conviction overturned. In 1976, his death sentence was lifted and Tyler was resentenced to life in prison. He spent forty-one years in Louisiana State Penitentiary, Louisana, finally walking out a free man in April 2016.

Harlem Hellfighters: the nickname of the former 15th New York Army National Guard regiment that was made up of mostly African Americans. During the First World War, they were sent to fight with the French Army in Europe, and spent more time in combat than any other American regiment – and suffered the most losses. Two Harlem

Hellfighters earnt the *Croix de Guerre* from the French government for their bravery. Despite the regiment's record in battle, however, the soldiers returned home to the United States to face racism and segregation.

Harriet Tubman (29 January 1822–10 March 1913): born into slavery in Maryland, in the United States, Harriet Tubman escaped to freedom in the North in 1849. She eventually became the most famous 'conductor' on the Underground Railroad, helping hundreds of other slaves to escape. During the Civil War (1861–1865) she nursed injured soldiers, and served as a spy for the North. Afterwards, living in New York, she helped the poor and sick, and spoke out on equal rights for black people and women.

Jim Crow laws, the: a series of laws in the Southern United States that enforced racial segregation in schools, public places, such as restaurants and drinking fountains, on public transport, in the armed forces and elsewhere, until 1965. The phrase 'Jim Crow' has often been attributed to 'Jump Jim Crow', a song-and-dance routine making fun of black people performed by white actor Thomas D. Rice in 1832. Soon, 'Jim Crow' became an insulting expression meaning 'negro'.

John Brown (9 May 1800–2 December 1859): born in Connecticut, John Brown was a white American who was strongly opposed to the institution of slavery in the United States. He believed in action rather than words, and he and his supporters carried out a number of violent raids, including one on the federal armoury at Harper's Ferry, Virginia, in 1859. He had intended to supply weapons from the armoury to local slaves, but was captured, hastily put on trial for treason against the Commonwealth of

Virginia, and hanged. At his own request, his body was then transported to his home near Lake Placid, in upstate New York, for burial. The property was declared a National Historic Landmark in 1998.

Juneteenth: also known as Freedom Day, this is an annual celebration on 19 June honouring the day when slaves were legally freed in the United States in 1865. Although Abraham Lincoln signed the Emancipation Proclamation on 1 June 1963, many slaves weren't actually freed. In Texas, around 250,000 people were still being held in slavery when, on 19 June 1865, Union troops arrived to tell them they were now free.

Ku Klux Klan (KKK): an extremist secret society in the Southern United States, set up after the Civil War, that has used violence to attack and frighten black people, preventing them from enjoying basic civil rights. Members hide their identities by wearing white robes and hoods and often use a burning cross as a symbol of their organization.

Montgomery Bus Boycott, the (5 December 1955–20 December 1956): a civil rights protest during which African Americans refused to use city buses in Montgomery, Alabama, as a protest against segregated seating. Four days earlier, on 1 December 1955, Rosa Parks, an African-American woman, had been arrested and fined for refusing to give up her bus seat to a white man. In 1956, the Supreme Court declared Montgomery's segregation laws on buses illegal.

Nelson Mandela (18 July 1918–5 December 2013): born in South Africa, Nelson Mandela was a member of the African National Congress party (ANC) and led both peaceful protests and armed resistance against the white minority government's apartheid regime. His actions landed him in prison for nearly thirty years. Released in 1990, he became the first black president of South Africa, forming a government of all races to become a champion for peace and social justice around the world.

Reverend Dr Martin Luther King Junior (15 January 1929–4 April 1968): born in Atlanta, Georgia, Reverend Dr King was an African-American Baptist minister who became a famous leader of the civil rights movement in the United States. He helped to organize a number of non-violent protests, including the Montgomery Bus Boycott in 1955, and those in Birmingham, Alabama, in 1963, and the March on Washington in the same year, where he delivered his electrifying 'I Have a Dream' speech. He was shot dead at the Lorraine Motel in Memphis, Tennessee, in 1968, which is now the site of the National Civil Rights Museum.

Rosa Parks (4 February 1913–24 October 2005): born in Tuskegee, Alabama, Rosa Parks grew up during the era of segregation, meaning that African Americans like her were forced to live separately from the white community. Her famous refusal to give up her seat on the bus to a white man led to the Montgomery Bus Boycott. Despite a change in the law, she received many threats from those who disagreed with her, and bomb attacks took place on the houses of various civil rights leaders, including that of Dr Martin Luther King Junior. After that, Rosa and her husband, Raymond Parks, decided to move to Detroit in Michigan. She continued to attend civil rights meetings and became a powerful symbol to many African Americans of the fight for equal rights.

Segregation: the action of setting certain groups, such as people from different racial backgrounds, apart from others.

Sergeant Stubby (1916–16 March 1926): a bull terrier or Boston terrier, Sergeant Stubby was the official mascot of the 102nd Infantry Regiment of the US Army, and was assigned to the 26th (Yankee) Division during the First World War. He saved his regiment from surprise mustard gas attacks in the trenches in France, located the wounded, and once caught a German soldier by the seat of his trousers, holding on to him until American soldiers arrived. He was awarded more medals than any other service dog of the First World War.

Underground Railroad, the: neither underground nor a railway, this was a secret network of routes and safe houses (known as 'stations') that was set up in the early to mid-1800s to help African-American slaves escape from the plantations of the Southern United States, to freedom in the North, or Canada and Nova Scotia. Individuals, known as 'conductors', would help the fugitives from one 'station' to another, under cover of darkness. Supporters of the cause, who were opposed to slavery and helped by donating money, food and clothing, were known as 'stockholders'. It is believed that approximately 100,000 slaves managed to escape this way.

Universal Declaration of Human Rights, the (UDHR): adopted by the United Nations General Assembly in Paris on 10 December 1948, this landmark document set out, for the first time, thirty fundamental human rights to be universally protected. Article 1 reads: 'All human beings are born free and equal in dignity and rights.' It has been translated into more than 500 different languages and is considered to be the basis of international human rights law.

Walk to Freedom march, the: a civil rights demonstration that took place on 23 June 1963 in Detroit, Michigan, attended by more than 125,000 people who were protesting against segregation and inequality between the races. Starting on Woodward Avenue, the protesters marched on to Jefferson and finished up at Cobo Hall Arena, where civil rights leaders gave rousing speeches to the crowd. The Reverend Dr Martin Luther King Junior was among the speakers, and the end of his address containing a more detailed version of his 'I Have a Dream' speech that he gave two months later in Washington.

Acknowledgements

One of the things I love about my job as a writer are the other people, and animals, involved in the creation of a published book. I was delighted to have Emma Jones as my editor once again, as well as copy-editors Stephanie Barrett and Mary O'Riordan, and proofreader Jennie Roman. Gift Ajimokun was a very welcome new addition to the editorial team for this book and had lots of additional information and insights to share. My research was greatly helped by the generous staff of both the New York and Detroit Public Libraries. Thank you.

Cute little Howly on the front cover and the chapter heading illustrations were once again thanks to Angelo Rinaldi and Emily Smyth. On the PR and marketing side of things I'm looking forward to the book tour with Louise Dickie and Beth O'Brien, as well as the welcome return of the sales experts Kat Baker and Lexy Mennie, and foreign rights manager Susanne Evans.

As always huge thanks must go to my agent and friend of almost twenty years, Clare Pearson.

One of the many lovely aspects of being a children's writer is visiting schools in the UK and abroad, but Emerson Valley deserves a special mention. The names of the winners of the writing competition held there – Robin, Joshua, Harry and Olivia – are included as characters in the book and in a happy moment I said I'd put other children (and staff) in the back if they'd like. So here they are: head teacher Sohelia Mathison, teacher David Caswell, three Charlies, Abduljabbar, Chloe, Phillip, Jack, Aldo, Joel, Jessica, Marissa, Ella, Tanisha, Martyna, Alex, Hizqil, Anest, Samuel, Alfie, Amina, Matipa, Bravinth, Mason, Minudi, Graziella, Adam, Dalia, Oliver, Megan and Salman.

Our golden retriever, Traffy, used to love being a reading assistance dog and her weekly visits to our local school. As soon as she realized where we were going she'd just about pull me into the school and, like Howly in this book, she had her own 'reading room', beautifully decorated by Karen Hales, with photos and children's drawings of Traffy and an endless supply of yummy treats. My other two golden retrievers, Bella and Freya, are also very partial to treats and have been demonstrating how to be a helpful dog in numerous ways during our school visits.

Beautiful Bella has recently been diagnosed with serious health issues and we've been told to treasure the next few months. So, with smiling faces and weeping hearts, we've been visiting her favourite places – the lake and the river and the woods. When I asked her oncologist if she could go to the beach he replied 'Oh, I insist on it!', which made me smile.

As Bella heads towards Rainbow Bridge, I am more grateful than ever for my husband Eric's support. He's busy making tasty tempting food for our girl while she's on our bed next to me, fast asleep and snoring softly, with Freya on the other side of her.

Researching and writing this book has been a fascinating learning experience, a study of many brave people determined to

help others and make things right, a true
voyage of discovery – sometimes sad but often
happy – and I very much hope you enjoy
reading it.

Author's Note

Researching and writing this book has been a truly fascinating and colossal learning experience. There was so much to discover I ended up bookmarking over five hundred websites and am still finding more to read every day. The terrible treatment of indigenous people by Christopher Columbus, the bravery of little Ruby Bridges, I could go on and on . . . Some of the books I found very helpful when writing this story were:

Parks, Rosa with Jim Haskins, *Rosa Parks: My Story*, Puffin Books, 1992

Theoharis, Jeanne, *The Rebellious Life of Rosa Parks*, Beacon Press, 2013

Orloff, Judith, 'Interview: Rosa Parks on the Power of Love', *Positive Energy*, Three Rivers Press, 2015

I decided to set the story in 1990 because it was the year of Nelson Mandela's release from prison and his meeting with Rosa Parks. By some oversight she wasn't invited to greet him when he arrived at Detroit Metropolitan Airport but Judge Damon Keith insisted she be there too. Nelson Mandela came off the plane to a cheering crowd, and when he saw Mrs Parks he began walking toward her, chanting 'RO-SA PARKS! RO-SA PARKS!' and the two seasoned freedom fighters embraced.

Also, the Rosa and Raymond Parks Institute for Self Development had recently been set up in 1987, the now well-established schemes using reading assistance dogs and school therapy dogs were being trialled, and the American Kennel Club's Canine Good Citizen award had begun.

The Birwood Wall in my story runs along the playground's edge at a fictional Elementary school. In reality, the wall – sometimes known as Detroit's Wailing Wall, Detroit's Berlin Wall or the Eight Mile Wall – runs for half a mile and cuts through a park and along the back of houses. In 1990 the wall wasn't decorated but nowadays some of it is painted with bright murals, and people and groups like Chazz Miller, P.A.W.Z. (Public Art Workz) and the Detroit Blight Busters, as well as many others, are working to create urban landscapes of beauty.

The Gateway to Freedom Monument didn't exist in 1990 at the time of my story. It was dedicated in 2001 and sculpted by Edward Dwight. It commemorates the role of the Underground Railroad in helping slaves to freedom and depicts eight figures getting ready to cross the river. George de Baptiste, one of the many amazing and brave people that there simply wasn't space to include in my story, is at the centre, pointing a finger toward Canada. On the other side of the river, in Windsor, Canada, there's the second half of the sculpture, the Tower of Freedom.

The Birmingham Children's March by thousands of African-American children in 1963 helped to put an end to segregation. Today children of every race are coming together for causes they care about. Hundreds of thousands of children are marching to protest about climate change and put an end to the destruction of the planet, trying to save our world for future generations. Rosa Parks, I have no doubt, would have been marching too.